Padraic O Conaire

15 Short Stories
Translated from the Irish by

CON HOULIHAN
JOHN JORDAN
DONALL MacAMHLAIGH
TOM MacINTYRE
BRYAN MacMAHON
JOHN McARDLE
THOMAS McCARTHY
VAL MULKERNS
THOMAS MURPHY
REDMOND O'HANLON
DIARMUID O MUIRITHE
SHEILA O'SULLIVAN
EOGHAN O TUAIRISC
EITHNE STRONG
NIALL TOIBIN

First published 1982 by Poolbeg Press Ltd.,
Knocksedan House, Swords,
Co. Dublin, Ireland.

Cover and design by Steven Hope.

Printed by Cahill Printers Limited,
East Wall Road, Dublin 3.

Contents

My Little Black Ass

translated by Eoghan O Tuairisc

It was in Kinvara I first got to know my little black ass. It was a fair-day and there he stood by the ditch with his backside to the wind, heedless of the world and the world of him.

But he caught my interest at once. I needed an ass. I was tired travelling on foot. Wouldn't he carry me and my bag and overcoat and all that? And who knows, I might get him cheap enough.

I inquired for the owner, but I had to search the town before I found him. He was outside a publichouse singing for pennies.

Of course he would sell the ass! Why wouldn't he sell, if he got his price? Yes, his price, not a single penny would he take from me bar his price.

And of course only for the hard times he'd never part with him — no, never! A fine young ass fit to go twenty miles a day at his ease. Give him a handful of oats once a month and there wasn't a racehorse in the country fit to keep up with him — no, not even a racehorse.

We both went to have a look at the ass.

Oh how the tinkerman sang his praises! There was never an ass since the first ass came to Ireland as mettlesome, as intelligent, as farsighted—

"D'you know a habit he has," he said admiringly, "if

you gave him a scrap of oats in the morning he'd put some of it aside for fear it might be scarce the morning after. There's not a word of a lie in that — not one word."

Somebody laughed. The tinkerman turned on him.

"What are you laughing at, you halfwit? He's that intelligent that he sets some of his oats aside. Isn't it often enough I was so short myself that I had to steal a little of his? Only for that ass we'd often go hungry — myself and my twelve daughters. . . ."

I asked whether he could distinguish between what belonged to his master and what belonged to the neighbours.

"He's as innocent as the priest," the fellow said. "If every beast was like him there'd be no need for ditch, fence, wall or dyke — no need at all."

By this time a big crowd had gathered. His own children were there — I don't know if the whole twelve of them were present, but as for those that were, it would be hard to find such a dirty ragged unkempt flock of children in any other spot in Ireland, and each one of them more impudent than another. His wife was there. Barefoot, bareheaded, wild. . . .

She broke into the discussion.

"Peter," she said to her husband, "d'you remember the day he went swimming into the river and brought poor Mickileen to land when he was getting carried off by the current?"

"Why wouldn't I remember it, Sive?" said he. "Yes, and the day I was offered five pounds for him—"

"Five pounds," she told me, "he got five pounds for him, five golden sovereigns into the heel of his fist—"

"On my oath I did," he said interrupting. "I had the money there in my fist and the bargain made—"

"But when he saw the poor ass," said she, "in tears

because we were parting with him, all he could do was renege the bargain."

"Ssh!" he said. "Speak easy I tell you. He understands every word we say. Look how he cocks his lug."

I offered a pound for this remarkable animal.

"A pound!" cried the tinkerman.

"A pound!" said his wife.

"A pound!" said the twelve daughters all together.

How astounded they all were. They gathered about to gaze at me. One child took hold of my coat, one took hold of my trousers, the youngest took hold of my knee.

Another one of them put a hand in my trousers pocket. Of course the creature was merely looking to see if I had even the pound — but instead of the pound she got a box in the ear, and not from the gentleman of the roads either. . . .

I was quite taken with the little black ass. He'd do. He'd carry me part of the road. And I could sell him whenever I might be tired of him.

"A pound," I repeated.

"Two pound," said the tinker.

"Oh woe, woe!" said the wife, "my fine ass sold for two pound!" And she began to wail and weep.

"For a pound," I said.

"For a pound — and sixpence each to the children."

The bargain was settled at that. I gave him the pound. I gave a sixpence to each one of his children round me. Then the wife began to call for Johneen and Eameen and Tomeen and the Lord knows how many more. There wasn't a beggar at the fair who didn't bring me his children all demanding and clamouring. The uproar they made! The tangle, the tussle, the hullaballoo all round me! One saying he got ne'er a penny while hiding the silver sixpence under his tongue. Another saying — but who could tell what anyone was saying or trying to say, there was such a bedlam about me.

What a pity I didn't give him the two pounds straight off and not bother with the gratuities!

I left town in fine style. Myself on the ass's back, the tinker gripping the halter on the right, his wife gripping it on the left, the flock of children surrounding us yelling their heads off.

Some of the town boys followed us, each of them giving me his own particular advice. The ass was compared to the most celebrated racehorses of the day; I was told to watch out or he'd take to his heels and never be seen again; I was advised to give him this food and that food — apparently the sight of myself on my little black ass escorted by the tinkers was the biggest lark of their lives.

But what did I care? Hadn't I got the ass, having long wanted such a four-footed beast?

Is it possible to describe how the ass and I parted with the tinkers? Nine times one after the other they all shook my hand; they all spoke to the ass softly, gently, coaxingly, endearingly. . . . Seven times over they recounted his qualifications. I was made promise to be kind and good to him, to give him a little fistful of oats when I could afford it, and if I valued my soul not to use a stick on him . . . .

Then as we parted they raised the lament. The father began it. The mother joined in. The children took it up, filling all the surrounding wood with the thin sharp wailing they made.

At last I was alone, myself and my little black ass.

He went at a gallop until we had left the wood behind. I had made an excellent bargain I thought: where would you find an ass with the speed of my little black ass?

But when we had left the wood behind it was a different story. He wouldn't stir a foot. I tried coaxing and enticing him with endearing words. He paid no heed. I thought to shift him by using the stick. Not an inch would he budge, he just stood there in the dead centre of the road.

People passed, some of those who had been at the fair and were now more than a little merry. I was advised to do this with him, do that with him, but when one of them advised me to carry him a bit of the way I lost my patience and threw a shower of stones after the fellow.

In the end I had to get down from his back and, yes, pull him along behind me against the drag of his legs and head . . . .

How handsomely I prayed for the tinkerman who had sold me such a beast!

But 'ere long I noticed a peculiar thing. He was skittish and nothing frightened him as much as the musical sound made by the wind through the branches of a tree.

As soon as he came under the branches of trees lining the roadside he always lost his stubbornness and could hardly be held. First he would cock a listening ear, then he'd shake himself like a dog coming out of water, then before you knew where you were he was off at a gallop. Right, said I.

I tied him to a gate, went into the wood and, getting an armful of fresh foliage, made it into a wreath which I fastened round his neck and up above his ears as we emerged from the wood.

Poor animal! He went at an incredible rate. He imagined from the music in his ears that he was still in the wood.

When we reached Ballyvaughan all the townspeople

came out to see the wonder — myself and my little black ass wearing his crown of leafy branches . . . .

I still have the little black ass and will till he dies. We have gone many a long mile together in rain and drizzle, frost and snow. He has lost some of his bad habits in the course of time — something I failed to do myself. And I think my little black ass knows that as well as anyone .

But he is as proud as punch since I bought him the little bright-green cart. Getting younger he is, poor beast!

The Woman on whom God laid His Hand

translated by Tom MacIntyre

A finer boat than the Cailin Beag Donn you wouldn't see in Galway Bay, and, as the shopkeeper who owned her was about to sell her, Padraig O'Nea thought she would make a good dowry for his daughter — if he could get her reasonably cheap. Anthony O'Malley, however, the young woman's intended, said that they'd be well advised to test the boat before buying, to discover if she came up to her reputation. The old man thought this good advice, and he and his son Seamus and O'Malley went out for a night's fishing to see what the boat was made of.

Kate, the engaged daughter, went to the quay with her people to see them off, and stayed a good while on the rise watching the fishing fleet go down the bay before the wind. It was late evening as she returned home, and her mother had supper prepared. The table was set and a cake cooling on the window-sill and the kettle was singing pleasantly. The two women sat at the table, gazing from time to time through the window at the boats which strongly resembled a flock of nuns taking the air in their convent garden.

It was growing very quiet. The birds — all lively music an hour before — were turning listless. It seemed that they'd tired of song and would never sing again. Birds and beasts were yielding to sleep but the young woman stayed at the window until the boats vanished from her in the darkness and a bright star showed fitful in the western sky.

The old woman by the fire sighed.

"What's wrong, mother?" Kate asked, rising and going to her.

"I'll be very lonely without you, dear."

"Won't you have my father, not to speak of Seamus?"

"Seamus won't stay long with us. There's nothing with the young people today only leaving."

"But how often you yourself made us laugh telling how you eloped with my father in spite of your people," Kate spoke encouragingly.

"And look at the life I've had since."

Her mother wasn't a complainer and the young woman was put out to find her thinking that way. She was well aware that her mother's people had been so opposed to her marriage that they hadn't spoken to her since. Her mother had a good upbringing and education but she'd gone with the life her husband had been able to give.

"But I'm not flying away from you," Kate said. "You'll see me often. I won't be more than twenty miles away."

"I know that, love," the mother replied, "but I've been thinking this while that my father's curse has followed me. Look how they've all left me — and now you. It seems to me they've left because I'm a little bit strange in myself now and again — isn't it said, 'to the seventh generation'?"

Kate took her mother's hand and caressed it. She knew well what was troubling her. She knew that there were few generations of her mother's people without one 'a little bit strange', and that some of them had been disturbed enough to require restraint. The local people weren't aware of that; her mother was from another county, and, if there was the odd one who'd heard the story, that wasn't pinning it down.

"You shouldn't talk like that," she said anxiously.

"But it's the truth, Kate," the old woman answered.

Night fell. Kate lit the lamp and drew the blind. Three visitors came, three not often seen together — Anxiety, Terror, and Hope. They were evident to the old woman by the fire, and she surprised her daughter when she threw the odd word into the talk of the visitors. To Kate, her mother was getting stranger by the day.

"The wind is rising, it's very dangerous on the sea tonight," the old woman remarked, her voice that of Anxiety.

The daughter let up the blind. There was a moon and the sea was altogether calm. It would never drown anyone again, it pronounced.

"Look, mother. Not a ripple. You're dozing."

The boat wasn't expected until daybreak.

"I'll stay here until morning," said the old woman, brooding. "Haven't a lot of people been drowned here in my time? Pat's Paddy and his people were drowned last year on a moonlit night just like this; and little Peg's Michael and his sister were drowned the year before last, and … was it two or three years ago the people of The Island were drowned?"

The mother was going on by the fire but her talk didn't worry Kate. Two better boatsmen than her father and O'Malley weren't to be had in the bay.

"Come here to me," the old woman said abruptly.

Kate went to her. The old woman took both her hands and gazed into her eyes.

"Kate, tell me the truth," she spoke. "If one — or two — from the boat were to be drowned tonight, whom would you wish to be saved?"

"For God's sake, mother, don't be talking like that," Kate answered, fearful, and she broke from her mother's grasp. The two sat by the fire, one each side. The old woman fell asleep and so did Kate. It was dawn when both were roused suddenly. Something heavy struck the closed door.

"Open the door," said the old woman calmly, "and we'll see which of them has come safe."

She had to open it herself — Kate sat there numb — and it was O'Malley who fell in a heap onto the floor, soaked wet, and terror in his eyes.

He was just able to tell the women his story. The boat had been wrecked at Carraganiolar. He had managed to get the old man ashore but the life was gone out of him. The young lad had an oar but there was no knowing what had happened there.

"Let us look for the bodies," said the old woman, going out.

*

The son's body was never found. The shore was searched from Loop Head to Galway but there was no sign of him. The father was waked but his wife never shed a tear.

Betimes she would be seen in some corner talking to a neighbour woman, and if you listened carefully you'd hear her words.

"This drowning is part of the old curse," she would say. "What's the point of tears? Isn't my heart too full for that? I always knew he'd be drowned one day."

She would go to the room where the body lay and — when alone there — speak to her husband.

"You often laughed about the curse, Patrick," she said to the corpse, "but, if the two of you are together now, tell my father to free me of it. Would you not tell him now, Patrick? I was always fond of you — from the first day I saw you — of your handsome head and your bright face."

She restrained herself when a neighbour came into the room, and, when the neighbour began to sympathise, she said only, "Stay quiet now. This drowning has to do with my father's curse. It was destined from the start. Kate is going too. In no time I'll be lonely as I was at the beginning."

She had to be sent off to rest before dawn.

After her husband's burial she turned stranger than ever. She would rise by night unknown to Kate and slip out and roam the shore searching for her son. She was often seen walking the shore by night, hair loose on the wind, wearing only her nightdress, keeping at it quite alone, searching every hole there was and striking her feet against the sharp stones. She spoke nonsense mostly but at times she sang verses. She had one never heard except from her.

It went—

I walk about at night
In rain and wind
Searching for my son, my treasure
Where are you from me, Seamus?

Then another thought would surface, and she'd say—

But when The Infant Jesus
Lay at the foot of The Cross
You were there, Mary
And He on your knee.

And she would say that her grief and hardship were far greater than Mary's because her son's body had not been returned to her after The Crucifixion.

"Where have you gone to, Seamus? Why aren't you on my knee?"

People who heard her going on like that would think of coaxing her home. Sometimes they succeeded. Sometimes they didn't and Kate would have the job of finding her.

She kept up the search and the night-walking until Kate had to sleep in the same bed with her. Even so, she awoke quite often to find the mother gone and the job there of going out to find her.

*

She was getting worse by the day. She lost her memory. Everything that had happened from her marriage thirty years ago was gone from her. If you mentioned her husband, she would reply that she had no husband but would shortly — in spite of her people. If anything was said of her family, she would reply that she had none: how could she since she had never married? She could, however, tell you precisely concerning all the events of her youth. She was in the habit of describing those days to Kate, imagining Kate to be her sister — the young sister dearest to her long ago. And Kate, heart-broken, had to listen to her and keep talk with her far into the night.

She went on most of all about her father. She would tell her 'sister' what he had said about the man she loved, how the two met at the fair, how he had abused the young man, and how the young man had struck him.

"And wasn't he wholly in the right?" she would say. "Hadn't he called him 'a rotten tramp'? But he'll come asking for me yet, and I'll elope with him in spite of them all, and you'll help me, Brigid, won't you now?"

You'd pity Kate listening to her mother describing vividly the father who'd been drowned, the mother imagining she was still young and about to marry him.

She didn't suffer a bad attack very often, however — perhaps a couple of times a month. When that happened, and Kate wasn't around, she would put on her wedding dress which she had laid by in a trunk and dress herself up in the fashion of the young women of thirty years back. If anyone met her, she would say that she had run away from her father, that she was dressed up for the man she loved, and that they would be together before the break of day.

It was a strange, grievous sight to see this old woman on whom God had laid His hand wandering the roads with her bright ribbons and her beautiful lace flowing in the breeze, and a sight more grievous again was the young woman on her trail, anxiously enquiring after her.

There was no evil, however, in the old woman on whom God had laid His hand. She was gentle towards all.

The neighbours pitied them both. The old woman had been 'a little strange' from the first day she'd come to the place. It wasn't thought that she'd quite lost her mind, that the same malady as had afflicted many of her people was now taking her. The neighbours didn't know enough about her background to arrive at that conclusion. If she was stranger than before, that was not surprising in the light of what she'd been through, the creature.

Kate, nevertheless, recognised the disease but kept her knowledge from the world. She didn't even tell it to O'Malley and it wasn't long before she regretted not having told him. At the start she had no desire to conceal it from him but, one day they were talking, he asked her if she thought it was that disease her mother had, and she answered that she didn't. And, at the time, that was true. But when she recognised the affliction she said nothing because that would have meant telling the whole story. She would have had to tell him all about her people, of her two uncles in the asylum, and of her aunt who hadn't left the house on her own for twenty years. She often spoke to her mother about the matter, and still more often considered it — until it seemed to her that the young man knew every bit as much about it as she herself did. What

would he say to her? The match would be broken off —
and how dearly she loved him — how did she know what
might happen? When they were married she would tell
him the whole story bit by bit. He would become accustomed to the ways of the woman on whom God had laid
His hand, he would have compassion for her and her
people when he understood the story. All things considered, it seemed better to postpone telling him.

About this time it occurred to Kate that it would help
the patient greatly if she were able to make a long visit
somewhere a distance from the sea. The boat had been
wrecked on a rock not far from the quay: that rock was
visible at low-tide, visible to the mother from the very
house: wouldn't it be much to her advantage if she were
to live somewhere well removed from that cursed sight?

Her elder married sister lived off in Mayo and the
young woman decided she couldn't do better than pay
her a visit. The sisters weren't as close as they might have
been, and, when Kate presented herself after the long
journey, the welcome wasn't particularly warm.

The sister and her husband kept a public house, and,
since they'd done better in the world than the people at
home, she concluded that Kate had come looking for help
— something she'd had to do before. She wouldn't have
come the journey without invitation unless that was the
reason.

The husband was serving in the shop, and the sisters
were left to themselves. Through a small window between
the room they were in and the shop, they could hear
plainly the voices of the men drinking.

"Well, Kate, and how's mother?" asked the sister.

"She's bad, Mary, very bad."

The sister was knitting but, from time to time she lifted
her gaze from the work, and affection and meanness could
be seen struggling in her eyes.

"She's worse?"

"Yes, much worse."

"Did she do anything strange lately?"

"She does something strange every day of the year."

Neither of them spoke for a little while. A young man, slightly drunk, could be heard singing in the shop.

"Every day that comes I'm in dread she'll do something terrible," Kate offered. "She only knows me the odd time now. She thinks I'm her sister, that I'm Brigid O'Donnell."

"God save us. And she hasn't seen Brigid in twenty-two years — since she married Dad."

The husband could be heard talking loudly.

"And Brigid and her husband are becoming very friendly to us," the sister continued after some reflection. "They were here the day before yesterday, they had tea with us very agreeably, and the captain said that he'd never — except once in India — tasted such tea."

"Bad luck to Brigid and the captain," Kate came back impatiently. "It isn't to talk about them that I made this journey."

An aunt married to an army captain was the topic. This couple never used the word 'aunt' or 'uncle' of the mother's people. They were important persons, in their own estimation, and would have nothing to do with the 'lesser' family. Neither of them had come to the funeral.

"Aren't you very impatient?" said the married sister. "But is she really bad every day?"

"No. Sometimes she has her right mind — but it's more pitiful to see her then than any other time."

Kate rose. Her voice turned bitter.

"Mary," she said, "my heart is breaking. Only God knows what I've been through this past year. I'm there in the kitchen with her, she sitting by the window, looking out at the sea, and such grief in her face as you never

saw. She wants to go away but she can't. Her eyes are
stuck to the place where that cursed rock is at the mouth
of the quay. Come the ebb tide, she sits there in her chair
by the window until the rock is visible. When she sees the
rock rising from the sea as the tide ebbs, she talks nonsense
to herself until mind and memory desert her.... It'd be a
great blessing if she could leave that awful place for a
long spell. I'm sure, Mary, she'd be happy to come to
you here for a space."

She fell silent to hear what her sister would say.

"Seven-and-sixpence," the husband spoke in the shop.
"Take it or leave it."

The sister said nothing for a long time. The stocking
she was knitting was on the table before her and her
spectacles beside it. Finally, she began to explain to Kate
why she couldn't take on the care of the mother. As it
was, the house was too small for them. There was no
room for her. They'd have to get her an attendant, and
money was scarce — a lot was owing to them. They had
a large family, and another child on the way. Thomas
had to be sent off to school somewhere, and that was
thirty pounds more a year....

And so on. Listening, Kate sickened.

"And besides, Mary," she spoke venomously, "the
shame of having the likes of her under your roof —
wouldn't the whole world know?"

The other woman rose in anger.

"People here would know of it, yes," she answered,
"but O'Malley who's going to marry you wouldn't. To
keep it from him you thought of getting rid of your poor
mother."

"No."

"Yes, I tell you. Afraid he won't marry you if he knew
the terrible disease our people carry."

"You lie."

"And you're a worse liar to claim you're here for your mother's good."

The hard words flashed between them like poison-tipped knives, they were both wounded, and Kate left the house with vengeance in her heart.

*

Hatred for the sister filled Kate as she departed. She made for the railway station but, since the last train was gone, she had to stay over in the town. She spent the night in an hotel by the railway and, long as she lived, she remembered that hotel and the night she passed there.

Lying on the bed fully-clothed, she got no sleep. She'd made the journey for the mother's good or so she'd thought leaving home. Thinking it over, however, through the night, she began to feel that maybe the sister wasn't altogether wrong; would she have come up with the plan at all were it not for the fact that O'Malley was coming to their village for the fishing season? Wouldn't he be in and out every hour of the day? Wouldn't he soon notice what was bothering her mother? And when he heard from her the story of her mother's people, what would he say — given the way she'd concealed it from the start? Wouldn't he detest her? And the way in which he was completely open with her?

The unhappy woman — in her burdened state — imagined that she'd come on the essential motive of her journey. She must have bad blood in her, no woman she'd ever known would do such a thing — to give her poor mother the road on account of a man.

Morning came, and she no longer remembered the rock on which her relatives were wrecked, nor the sea on which her mother's eyes dwelt on her better days, nor the terrible grief in those eyes, nor her own pity, nor the love between them. The hard word spoken was lodged in her heart. She felt herself the worst woman ever born.

But God and man grant forgiveness to the sinner who repents. She would repent. She'd never marry. She would stay at home looking after her mother and waiting on her till she died. Tomorrow when she'd meet O'Malley, she'd tell him the whole story. He'd hate her, doubtless, but perhaps, with the passing of time, he'd forgive her the deception, and in two or three years would he not be her friend again some other way?

The beautiful young woman sitting alone in a corner of the carriage was leaden-hearted as the train left the station. She understood that day why the prayer terms this lovely world a vale of tears.

*

Reaching her own town, she saw a scatter of people outside the house of John O'Neill, the magistrate. There was a car in the street, and a policeman holding the horse. Going by the house, she noticed that those present were looking keenly at her and that some wanted to speak to her but hesitated to make the move.

She hadn't gone far before she was called back, and she entered the house. There was her mother, the old wedding-gown on her but sodden and dirty, the once-bright ribbons and lace trailing about her as she sat on a chair singing a love-song.

O'Malley was present, and he explained the story to Kate. He said the mother had been taken bad that morning, escaped from the old woman in charge of her, and injured a neighbour-woman about to take her home. Now they were going to commit her.

Kate spoke to her but got no sign of recognition. She

was rambling, saying that she was very grateful to these good people — meaning the police — who were about to take her to the man she loved.

She recognised Kate, however, when she boarded the car — took Kate, rather, to be her own sister.

"I always trusted you," she said, "but you thought to keep me from him like everybody else. You failed. These good men came to my help. He sent them to me....

Oh, youth of the grey eyes
To whom I gave heart's love...."

those were the last words Kate heard from her as the car went over the road.

Kate and O'Malley went back to the house. They had two-and-a-half miles to go but not a word was spoken until they were almost at the quay. It was a fine pleasant evening and the birds were singing buoyantly in the trees. The fishing-fleet was going down the bay in full sail. If there's hardship and heartbreak in the world, you would think on such an evening that it's man's doing and not the will of God.

O'Malley wished to say something to the girl he loved but what could he say? In the end he had to speak.

"Have courage, Kate, love."

"I will."

"God laid a heavy hand on her."

"And a much heavier hand on those she left after her — but it's the will of God that we accept it."

There's a rock near the quay known as 'The Big Chair': as they were going past it, she said, "Let's sit here a moment, Anthony."

They sat there. He held her hand while she gazed at the sea, pondering.

"For two years I've often thought," she said — and it seemed to her she was speaking to herself, "often thought when she was having a bad turn that reason and understanding are no advantage — that loss of reason is preferable. She's easy tonight but my heart is black as coal and heavy as lead...."

The young man didn't rightly understand her.

"It's reason that has destroyed us," she said.

"But listen, Kate dear," he said. "Our lives haven't been destroyed. There's a grand life together before us with the help of God."

"No. I'll never marry."

"Never marry — why?"

"I deceived you, Anthony. I didn't tell you of the disease my mother had."

"But I knew myself. You don't talk of the like of that," said the young man, wonderingly.

"And I kept from you the condition of my mother's people, I never told you that she had two brothers in the asylum and a sister not much better than them...."

"What's wrong with you, Kate?" he asked. "Haven't I known that for years?"

She was surprised but she didn't question him. She burst into tears.

The sun was setting when they separated.

"No good in your talking to me — I'll never marry," was her last word that evening.

*

Nor did she marry. O'Malley came asking often but she wouldn't consent. She's still living in the cottage near the quay, often to be seen in the little window looking out on the sea and on the rock where her people were wrecked, waiting for the day when she'll be with her mother in heaven or in the asylum.

The Woman at the Window

translated by Sheila O'Sullivan

Someone outside was throwing sand at the window, trying to wake me. It wasn't my blessing that was bestowed on that person, I can assure you . . . .

I heard a voice outside, the voice of a woman. I recognised her voice, and at once became wide awake. Before you'd have finished saying "God save me" I was out on the floor; but I swear to you that I wouldn't have risen from that grand bed for any other voice in the world.

But she — who could fail her?

*

In to me came the Widow O'Hara, looking younger than I had seen her for many a day. No one would think that she was seventy-five, qualified to draw the Old Age Pension had she needed it, and that her daughter and grand-daughter, both widowed, live in one house with her.

"Put the donkey under the cart," said she.

I obeyed without question. You'd know that she was on some unusual exploit. Her old cheek was slightly flushed, a queer glint was in her eye. I've seen the same glint in the eye of a schoolgirl bent on playing some risky prank. I didn't discuss the cause of her gaiety with the old woman. I know her better than that: it's hard to extract a secret from her — but time would tell.

The pair of us set out on the donkey cart, I and the old woman with that secret gaiety in her heart.

*

The countryside all round was smiling with us: the bright autumn sun, rising high in the sky, was transforming glen and plain into a golden lake, and the wayside tree into a golden image; it cast showers of golden-yellow light on branch and twig and leaf so that you would think the golden age had come.

The donkey was going on at a trot: I was rejoicing in being alive and well on such a wonderful autumn morning; the old woman beside me was rejoicing too — but what cause for rejoicing had she, who had spent, and was still spending, a sad life?

And were it not for her light and youthful heart her life could indeed be termed a troubled one, with her husband dead before she was thirty, her sons in exile and struggling with the world, and her widowed daughter and grand-daughter living with her — three widows disagreeing and wrangling in the same house!

Only for having property of her own I suppose she couldn't be as youthful and hearty as she was . . . .

I looked closely at her as the two of us sat side by side in the little donkey cart on that bright autumn day. She was dressed in her Sunday clothes — a good gown of old black silk, a black old-time hooded cloak, a peaked bon-net, gold-rimmed spectacles — but you would hardly notice that because of the smile on her lips, the flush in her cheek, the unusual activity on which she was bent.

We passed the house in which she lived.

It was easy to note that she didn't want to be seen on the little donkey cart. She had an old umbrella of large proportions; she held it over her so that she wouldn't be recognised — of course the poor woman didn't realise that everyone in the parish was acquainted with that umbrella!

"I think I wasn't seen," said she when we were almost past the house.

"Indeed you weren't," said I, but I didn't tell her that she certainly had been recognised if anyone were at the window.

The donkey came to the untimely conclusion that he had done enough trotting for the day. He lowered his head, shook his scanty tail, and stood in the middle of the road.

I rose. . . . I gave him three or four belts of my blackthorn in the ribs. He moved only his ears, and wouldn't have moved his feet had I been at him ever since.

The old woman rose. She let him have the umbrella on the ribs on his left side, and both of us kept on lashing him till we were exhausted.

Then we had a consultation.

"We'd better walk," said she.

"Have we far to go?" said I.

"You'll know that soon enough," said she, and squeezed her lips together for fear her secret should escape from her.

We were going to alight when the donkey changed his mind. He shook his head. He flapped his ears. He moved his feet. Off with him at a gallop.

I couldn't pay any particular attention to the gay old woman beside me, but I knew she was excited, and delighted with the ride. Her heart was as young on that sunny autumn day as it had been on any day for fifty

years. If you were to see myself and the woman on the
donkey cart, with her arm round my waist for fear she
should fall, her fine Sunday bonnet cocked over one eye
from the swaying, a smile on her lips, a smile in her eyes,
the landscape round us smiling with us — were you to
see us, you could only conclude that I was abducting her!

Hadn't we fun and hadn't we sport, hadn't we com-
motion and hadn't we enjoyment, myself and the gay old
woman who had been a widow for over forty years!

She put a word in my ear.

"I'm going to do something to-day," said she, "that I
didn't do for fifty years — something I thought I'd never
do again. I'm hearty and brave today — my youth
returning. . . ."

We were at the gate of a corn field. She made me halt
the spirited donkey, and we alighted.

*

The corn was in stooks. She told me to load the cart, and
helped me vigorously and excitedly the while.

I knew that the field and the corn belonged to the
daughter, being part of the considerable property left to
her by her husband when he died. But what was the old
woman up to? Hadn't she plenty labourers about the
place to bring home a load of corn if it were needed? And
what did she mean by "doing something today she hadn't
done for fifty years"?

The cart was laden with the corn. Out the gate with
us. The donkey was trying to make for home. She pre-
vented him.

"Where are we off to now?" said I.

"To the market — to Kilronan to sell the corn."

I was astounded. She didn't need the money, and here
she was going off to the market — she, a rich woman, a

proud woman — with a mean little load of corn. What on earth ailed her? Why had she been so excited since morning?

I was bewildered. . . .

We sold the corn.

She led me into a tavern. She was known there, and the two of us were conducted to a private room. Two glasses were placed before us. She tasted the wine, and grew pensive.

"Fifty years," said she, "fifty years today! Isn't it a long spell!"

She fell silent. I did not disturb her.

"For fifty years I never did such a thing," said she, and you'd think that it was with herself she was communing, "and I thought I'd never do it again. To steal a load of corn, to sell it and spend the money with a man in an inn. . . ."

She looked closely at me.

"And you're very like him in the forehead," said she, "though he was a finer-looking man than you. . . . that man of mine. . . . fifty years today — we weren't married then — we went off to the market with a load of corn. We spent the money in this house. . . . I didn't think I'd ever do such a thing again. . . .but this morning when I called that day to mind I grew young again—"

She took my hand. Her old eyes were tearful.

"Fifty years! A health to that day! God rest his soul. . . ."

"Amen!" said I.

"You are very like him, very like him indeed," said the old woman, with a catch in her voice.

I did not speak. She squeezed my hand, and her eyes looked away, gazing sadly back across the years.

Tetrarch of Galilee

translated by Eithne Strong

I am truly pleased, Rhesa, my foster-son, at your coming to visit me in this filthy hovel I have in the wilderness. But remain some distance from me or you will have a heavy load of maggots and pests on your return to Jerusalem. Multiplying every day they are in spite of all I kill between those two flat stones! Notice the holes they have pitted in my flesh! Do not be terrified — is not human flesh eaten in the grave, and am I not a dead soul even though I was once king over the territory of Galilee?

Yes, my son, you wish me to talk a little with you; it is also my wish, it is so long since I spoke before this except to the vermin that forever consume me. . . .

I would still be a king in high degree and respected were it not for the women. In the history books it is said that every evil deed Herod Antipas, Tetrarch of Galilee, did, he did because of some woman. That is the truth, son: from the beginning of my life I could never stay away from them, being certain the while that they would cause my death. Why, then, did I dally with them, is it? You are, indeed, young! Destiny, no doubt: look at the butterfly yonder fluttering over my candle. It will not be long until its lovely wings are burnt; how do we know that it does not itself also know this?

You were extremely well acquainted with Salome, the daughter of my step-brother, Philip. You were. Had it not been for her I should not have compelled you to go into the army that time — listen to me, I say — soon you will understand what she had to do with your soldiering! But you knew her. You did, and you loved her. It's very well I remember the day when the two of you were disporting yourselves on the sward in front of the house. The weather was fresh then. Orange and almond trees were blossoming and the whole world was joyful after the inclemency of winter. But as I watched you through the window I thought that there was nothing in this beautiful world so beautiful as you two. . . .

You put the girl dancing on a flagstone. I did not wonder at your delight in watching her. But her shoe fastening came undone. She fell. You lifted her up carefully. You kissed her on the mouth. She blushed. She pouted — you remember her laughing mouth? But the look that came into her eyes! "I dare you to do it again!" was what was perfectly plain from that look. And you didn't do it! You were young and little you knew about the language of the eyes. All you'd need now, you rogue, is the chance.

But her features took on a completely different expression as she went past the window when she had parted from you. A peculiar look, that look. It is a rare person sees it for the first time in a woman's face. Joy comes into the heart of him who does see it, ideas come into his mind. . . .

"Salome is no longer a child now," I said to myself, "but a woman, a beautiful nubile woman," and I began to think about the characteristics of women. . . .

While I was reflecting, who should come upon me but Herodias. Before I perceived her near me she laid a hand affectionately on the back of my head in her usual way. If I were to get back my kingdom for it, I could not tell you why I rudely cast the hand from me. But Herodias understood why I did it: did you ever see a flash of hell in a woman's eyes, Rhesa? You never did. You are not at all better for it. But this woman frightened me to the core.

"I didn't think it was you there," I said, clumsily enough.

"And you wouldn't recognize my hand beyond that of any other woman!" she said. "If it's getting tired of me you are. . . ."

I swore it was not so. I swore it on the seven great oaths. I impressed it on her with thousands of kisses and embraces. Did she believe me? How did I know? Women have greater intuition in these things than we do. They know that a man is getting tired of them before the man himself knows. That is a gift of theirs. At any rate Herodias pretended she believed every word from my mouth.

"You are my pet," she said — but what is the good my telling you, Rhesa, who are knowledgeable in these things, what a woman might say when she wants a favour? You know your foster-father very well: do you think he could refuse anything to a woman who would speak persuasively, lovingly, to him? Is it any great surprise to you that she was promised that the fool who used to preach and create disturbance throughout the country would be tied up in chains; neck, hands and feet? Oh yes, that's what he was called — John the Baptist. He was forever telling the people that I had done wrong in abducting and marrying my stepbrother's wife. I paid little attention to him and his nonsense but his talk wounded Herodias or she pretended it did. In truth, Rhesa, it was not about John, nor Herodias, nor Aretas, the father of my first spouse and who was declaring war on me at that time — it was not about these I was thinking that night but about lovely ravishing Salome . . . . At any rate, John was seized and incarcerated in the bottom of a dry well at the top of that little garden we used to call the Garden of Peace.

Unless I am tiring you I'll tell you how matters were for me then. I loved Salome, my wife's daughter. I was sure of it. You know me; you know that I would not have another day's peace unless I had the woman I loved, body and soul. But what would I do with her mother, proud Herodias? Send her home to my stepbrother, to Philip? If I did that, if I were to take John's counsel, the whole populace would be on my side. To banish the woman I hated and make a saint of myself! This counsel pleased me, Rhesa — it would be very amusing if it were thought that Herod banished a woman from him because of any law. . . . But I would have to banish Salome too . . . .that was a thing that didn't please me. That was a thing I would not do. I could not banish Herodias without banishing Salome also. A serpent in the house is a bad thing: that woman was sharper, more poisonous than any serpent. Women's hatred amazes me. . . .

And Aretas — wasn't he the madman, Rhesa? — Aretas was declaring war on me because of his own daughter, the first wife I ever had; you did not know her at all, son — the tiniest loveliest feet you ever saw, but . . . .no matter; little value I placed on her when I first set eyes on proud Herodias. And you, yourself, Rhesa: I was afraid Salome loved you from the day I saw you in the Garden of Peace. That caused me no anxiety or bother however. I knew the love-bond (if such existed) would be undone if the two of you were separated. I sent you away from each other. You, Rhesa, I sent to the battlefield, hoping you would not return. . . . Are there not innumerable worries and difficulties to afflict a man who loved one woman yesterday, loves another woman today, and will love another tomorrow? The disease affecting me was noticed. Don't you remember a satire made by a wandering poet who used to travel the country at the time? The scum of the city used to mouth it as I went past in my chariot.

Are you not young, asking me such a question! Why didn't I banish the pair of them? Why didn't I make a settlement with my enemies, with the father of my first wife and with the Jewish people? The love I had in my inmost heart for Salome. . . .but don't think I didn't do my utmost to extinguish that love. I took a good deal of the advice given to people in such a situation, that sound advice to be had in the eighteenth chapter in the book of Elijah's philosophy. I was occupied from morning till night. Affairs of government which I had neglected for some time, I attended to. I went ahead boldly with the war. I did not speak to Salome but it was a rare night I did not have women in my company to entertain me. You remember the troupe of dancing women the Emperor gave me — and there were beautiful women amongst them, women who were brownskinned, full-limbed, round-breasted, great-eyed. There was no use in it, however. There are the two sorts of love, as you know, physical love and spiritual. I gave the first kind to the dancing women, and to other women besides, but I gave to Salome both, and you know yourself that there is no cure for him who gives both kinds of love to a woman. You are not sure, is it? I was not sure of it once. But I am now.

Yes, I did my best. I followed the counsel almost totally — foreign women, magic wines from Arabian districts, hard work — many a time I spent a long day digging in the fields, books — I read a great many books of Greek philosophy — but if I heard Salome laughing I flung from me whatever I was engaged upon to go and look at her. . . .

I gave a feast one night. At Machaerus I was at the time, and that was where I had John imprisoned. Leaders of the army, court nobles, and government administrators were there, and all of them merry, festive. There were wines and I thought they would have the virtue to banish my heart's torment. Wine from Tyre was there, the colour of enemy blood; one goblet of it was enough to induce an urgency to battle — among my friends I divided this. There was wine from the mountains of Moab; the property of this wine was that you felt no pain having drunk it — it did not cure the pains of love, Rhesa. That wine given to me by the Emperor when he was progressing through, that wine was the colour of the waves of Galilee on a winter's day — the wine of insight it was called, because one drop of it revived whatever intelligence a man ever possessed: I did not drink it. There was the wine of love — purple wine which came from Greece; while this wine was being made it was mixed with the blood of seven maidens who loved a man; I did not require the wine of love. . . .

It was little I, myself, drank of any of these wines. I knew Herodias was somewhere behind the screens thinking out some plan to confound me. If I could enrage her! If I could insult her before the gathering! I summoned the troupe of dancing women presented me by the Emperor. They came in, eight of them, eight brown-skinned half-naked women slaves, and they performed a barbarous dance before the assembly.

There was one particular woman, a little rounded agile woman, and I compelled her to do a special dance. She drooped herself, she undulated, she curved and bowed, sometimes walking on air, yet again totally still, a brown marble column; there was no twist nor turn ever achieved by the human body that she did not execute with her body to entertain the inebriated men who were all about her, praising her.

"However excellent she is," I said, "there is another dancer in the house who has surpassed her."

Those assembled were suspicious. Nobody spoke.

"The other dancing woman," I said, "is the cleverest and most beautifully made woman, with the fairest skin, the loveliest foot, the blackest eye, the most even teeth. She has royal blood in her veins. Her movements are more entrancing than the light of the moon dancing on the sea of Galilee. The berry of solace is not redder than her lips. Her eyes are the smooth dark marble of Mount Jerome in the brilliance of the sun after rain. From the blackbird she stole her voice. The woven tresses of her thick hair is as the writhing of hundreds of serpents in dumb pain. . . ."

I looked around on the gathering of men. There was not a stir from anyone but their eyes all fastened on me while they wondered what trick I was about to play. Herodias was also listening to me but I didn't see her: to degrade that woman whom once I loved and cherished, that was what I wanted — if I could persuade Salome to perform a particular Arab dance in front of the lascivious drunken men present, would not that be a dire insult to both? How did I know, might it not even diminish my love? I had a notion that I might not yearn any longer for her if she were to do the barbaric dance she exulted in, before the men. . . . Have you ever noticed, Rhesa, what a tremendous temptation a man experiences to subjugate the woman he loves? You have, of course; that temptation comes when the woman has too much power over him.

I went outside. The moon was risen, the colour of blood. The mournful bittern was screeching dismally in the wilderness, the wolf menacing in the mountains of

Moab. But I was much more interested in the sounds of the man I had incarcerated at the bottom of the well in the Garden of Peace. Something of what he said came to me on the wind:

"My curse on you. . . .my curse on the man who abducted the wife of his stepbrother. . . .may they have no issue. . . .the wanton who offended the God who created her with lust of the flesh. . . .but her day will come. . . ."

He had a wonderful voice, a strong intense voice with as many shades and modulations as there are colours in the rainbow. His voice pleased me greatly. I went to the well where he was. As I neared the well I saw eight or nine people slipping away from me in the darkness. I remembered that I had given permission to some of his followers to visit him every other day: was it not pleasant instruction he was giving them? But I, myself, was indifferent. . . .

One of the soldiers there lowered a rushlight at the end of a chain into the dry well and it was an astonishing sight we saw. A tall slender spare barefoot man with camel skins about him as a covering. He was pale, exhausted, the mark of hunger and danger in his noble countenance while he hurled bitter denunciations at me, every word as sharp and destructive as a Roman spear. But the two eyes in his head! And the look he turned on me! He could not have looked at me with greater loathing and abhorrence if every evil spirit that ever walked the earth was in my body. Isn't it fearful the manifestation people assume because of religion, Rhesa?

An idea occurred to me. There was a feast taking place inside; did I not have an obligation to give the guests the greatest diversion possible? I spoke to a soldier. He bowed his head. I, myself, went inside.

I met Herodias near the door, thunderclouds on her brow.

"Woman, let Salome be arrayed for dancing," I said.

"It will be done, O Tetrarch," and she departed.

I went into the gathering. I did not tell them the amusement I had conceived for them. A woman slave stretched a goblet of wine towards me. There were two trained peacocks in the middle of the floor, their keepers urging them to do particular tricks. An attendant came to the door. Another attendant spoke to me.

"Let him be brought in," I said.

A man whose covering was camel skins was brought in, five soldiers surrounding him. Those gathered laughed on seeing this man. Some were about to jeer him. I did not allow them.

"Even if he is a prisoner let him celebrate with us tonight. Let him be given wine and delectable food," I said.

He was offered the food and drink. He did not taste them.

"He'd prefer locusts from the wilderness, and honey from the wood, and insipid water from the river Jordan to your food, O Tetrarch," said a young Roman near me.

The Roman was a jester. He also had drunk plenty of the wine. He stood up. He put a brass helmet on the prisoner's head. He tied a sword to his waist. He fastened a Roman breastplate around him. He sang a battle song telling everyone that henceforth they would have no other army leader but this. . . .

More wine was drunk. The bawdiest songs were sung, the most obscene stories told, but over the noise and confusion the prisoner was to be heard all the time praying and saying: "My curse on you, O Tetrarch of Galilee. My curse on the whore you have for a wife. The Son of God will come in anger. The hand of the Son of

God is heavy. He will fell his enemies. They will be banished to outer darkness. Their progeny and the progeny of their progeny will be ground between the millstones of the two worlds. . . ."

Wasn't I patient not to strangle him? But his talk caused me no unease — I never had any offspring!

It was then she came to me, the beautiful daughter, Salome of ill-fate. She was never shy, but you would imagine by her as she was coming across the floor while all the men looked, fascinated, at her, that never was there so shy a woman in the world. I was in a little recess by myself, and she moved slowly towards me, she sat at my feet, she put her two hands around my knees and gazed piteously up into my face like someone who might be about to ask a favour.

"I am ready, O Tetrarch, but do not ask me to dance," she said.

I realised she was looking delectable and I suspected she knew her beauty could move me. Was I not idiotic to think she was ashamed to dance before this concourse of men? She had intended from the start to dance. All she wanted the whole time was to entice me, to tantalise me with her loveliness at her mother's insistence so that I would grant her the favour they both wanted. She was the cat and I was the mouse, while I all the time was convinced she was under my control and authority!

"I shall dance for you and for the company, O Tetrarch, but there will be no spring in my feet, no grace in my movement. . . ."

Did you ever meet someone, Rhesa, who was in two minds when he should be firmly in one? It was so with me when the girl spoke thus. To discredit her, to sully and insult her, to defeat her, to dominate her, to shame her, to set aflame hatred for her in my heart, it was for that I brought her here, so that henceforth I should be freed in mind, body and decision. But Rhesa, foster-son, do not blame me — when she turned towards me time to time and when I saw her cold white brow like the marble of the Lonely Mountain; and below that her large luminous eyes in which were the softness, sweetness and darkness of night; and her breast rising and falling rhythmically like the waves of the sea; and her soft moist mouth like a red rose just awakened on a dewy morning; and when I heard the voice coming from her mouth, a voice more musical, gentler, more pleasing than the sound of the thousands of white doves we both once heard in the coppice of a wood near Rome, Rhesa — yes, when I saw and when I heard those things, do you wonder that I was tempted? I did not yield to the temptation however. I didn't yield to all of the temptation I should say. If she were to ask me to release her at that moment I should have done it, I fear. Never request a half-favour. Salome requested a half-favour. She merely said: "I'll do the Dance of the Child for you."

"That is not what I want. The Arab dance you have been a month practising is what I want."

You know both dances, Rhesa. There would be no shame in dancing the first one. For that reason it would not suit me.

"The Arab dance I want."

"That dance! And to do it in front of those drunken men over there?"

"Yes."

"But the wine is gone to their heads and there is lust in their hearts. I should far prefer to stay here with you, O Tetrarch, talking and conversing and delighting your heart. . . ."

If she were not to do it of her own accord I could not compel her to do it. I thought to coax her.

"Anything at all you wish you will get if you perfrom the dance well."

She put on an air. Childish, she was, like a petted child trying to conceive what plaything she could ask of her mother. But alas! She most certainly knew the thing she wanted. Making a fool of me, she was. All the time she was pulling the wool over my eyes. Do not think, Rhesa, that you have ever triumphed over a woman until you see her in her grave. I promised her excess of jewels and gifts if she danced.

"The twelve serpents that the Queen of Syria gave me, you will have from me," I said. "Not one of them is the same colour, age, size, nor cleverness as the other. They are so trained that you may make of them a live multi-hued chain to wear around your waist as a belt. . . ."

She shook her head.

"I have eight dumb slaves: they are skilled in the eight ancient skills that have existed since the beginning of the world, that is to say magic, wizardry, poetry, agriculture, weaving, seafaring, praying and the making of oaths."

They did not please her.

"The magic swans in the Lake of Two Fishes in the country of Moab. . . ."

She despised them. She did not wish to do the Arab dance, it appeared, and no other dance would suit the occasion.

She looked directly at me and said:

"Let us both go out to the Garden of Peace and let us walk there under the beautiful almond trees which are now blossoming and kissing the earth with the weight of their load of loveliness: the moon is risen, majestic queen of the stars with diaphanous silver clouds as a mantle about her. The birds make harmony in the pomegranate trees, in the illusion that it is day because of the wonderful light from the stars and moon. . . ."

"The Arab dance I want," I said roughly to her. It was a tremendous temptation, Rhesa. Let me be praised that I didn't yield.

"Let us go out, O Tetrarch, and let us sit under the fig tree at the top of the Garden of Peace, and I will sing for you. I will sing you a love song that I was taught in Judea long ago; and while you are listening to that you will not be mindful of the bird music being sung all about you, nor of the fragrance of the trees, nor of the beauty of the night, nor of the worry of this life, nor of sorrow nor woe, you will be aware only of the song and the singer. . . . O Tetrarch, come on to the Garden of Peace with me, come on! Come on!"

I was silent a while. Two visions came before my eyes. The Garden of Peace. . . . Salome. . . .myself in a silken bond, in a love bond with her for ever and ever. . . . That, or me as authentic king. . . .she and her mother banished from me. . . .all the people helping me. . . .the country in my control. . . .

I heard the sounds of the men making merry in the Hall of Festivities. I heard the voice of John the Baptist mounting and receding while he cursed me: "His house will be burnt over his head. The savage tribes will come into his kingdom and stone will not be left on stone; there will be no child not crying; there will be no woman who will not tear out her hair cursing him. . . ."

"The dance! The Arab dance, Salome! You will get anything if you do it."

"But if I ask for the blind black eagle which your people had since the time of David?" she said innocently.

"You will get it. No matter what you ask, only do the dance. Have you not got my word as king?"

She got up and danced.

It was not at her I looked while she danced. It was not at the men who stared at her with lecherous eyes under heavy black brows. It was not at the prisoner who was covered with camel skins and, in ridicule, decked out as a Roman soldier — it was not at these I was looking, nor of these I was thinking but rather looked at and thought about a great wide kingdom from Dan to Beersheba, a kingdom that would be in my jurisdiction and power; I was thinking of fame, renown, dominion. . . .

The dance was finished. The woman came to me.

"Your request, woman," I said.

"The head of John the Baptist on a dish," she said.

It was clear she meant it. I realised that this was what she wanted all the time and that there was no use in my attempting to move her. She had my word.

I whispered to an attendant. The prisoner was led out. The woman followed him. The company renewed their festivities. A song had scarcely been sung by someone when Salome returned carrying the noble bloody head. . . .

The assembly slipped away from me one by one and I was left alone in the Hall of Festivities. . . .

Were you ever climbing in the midst of rough wild hills, tired, hungry and thirsty, hoping that you would succeed in finding shelter if your feet would carry you — and then upon reaching the place where you had hoped for help there was nothing to be seen but a deep black abyss that you were unable to cross? It was so with me that night. The great kingdom, the power, the fame, the renown I saw in my vision, they were scattered as a mist is scattered before the morning sun. . . .

It is appropriately you put the question, Rhesa: what business had a young girl like that with a bloody head like that, eh? It was not for herself she asked the favour. I did not know it that night but I know it now, alas! Numerous were the stories going about regarding the terrible doings of that night, and it is possible one of them reached the uncivilised regions where you lived for a long time; but don't believe any of them. . . . Patience, Rhesa. Let me tell it to you in my own fashion.

The assembly had scarcely gone away from me to leave me alone in the great dark Hall of Festivities, when Herodias came in. I did not show that I was frightened and disturbed because of the events of the night. You'd imagine from the woman that she had heard nothing at all about the beheading.

"Your life and health, O Tetrarch of Galilee!" she said smoothly and politely. "Was it not early the company left you? Was it that they did not like the Arab dance?. . . . Eugh! What's this? Blood? I do not like blood: order a servant to clean the floor. I find it astounding that a group cannot come together without fighting amongst them!"

"There was no fighting, O queen," I said. "That is the blood of a prophet."

"The blood of a prophet! I did not think there was any prophet in this country for many hundreds of years."

"That is the blood of someone you hated. That is the blood of John the Baptist who was always cursing you. He was beheaded tonight."

"I know that. Salome presented me with his head as she promised. . . . But you had no right to taint this fine hall with his blood."

"And Salome presented you with his head!"

"She did."

She was silent for a little while. A change of appearance came over her. She crouched on the floor like a wild animal guarding its portion. In the darkness all I could see was a white face and venomous eyes boring into me.

"His head was presented to me, O Tetrarch," she said, "but don't think I was looking for it because of his stupid words. Do not think either that I was at all afraid we

would be separated because of them. . . . I have a firmer
hold on you, O stupid man! And it is not for your good
I have this hold on you. For a long time it was not a bond
of love binding us but an unbreakable bond of hate. There
was a time. . . .but what good is it to talk like that? For
a year you were longing for my daughter. You had no
interest in me — yes, don't you remember the day you
flung my hand from you when I was meaning to be warm
and companionable with you? Since that day nothing was
bothering me day or night but how to plan the way for
your destruction. . . . You were longing for Salome during
that year. I, myself, was longing only for revenge. Salome
— she was the irresistible bait I had! I was ready to make
a sacrifice of her on the altar of revenge — if necessary.
But now I have won, O Tetrarch of Galilee. Your enemies
are powerful, not only in this country but in Rome and
in Jerusalem. Increasing in bulk, power and number they
will be because of the work of this luckless night. . . ."

There were only two small torches in the room. A
window was broken with a stone. One of them was
extinguished.

"Increasing they will be, O Tetrarch. Do you not hear
John's followers angry and threatening even now? Now
since he is dead they will help your enemies, the king of
Petra who is making war on you, and all of them. You
know about the Jewish people, Essenes, Pharisees, and
all of them that are there. You have no hostage now with
which to control them. They will come on you in their
tens of thousands, armed and furious. . . .and there will
be people in Rome to whisper in the ear of the Emperor
and who will be believed; do you think the Emperor will
not believe you are mad and that slaughter and turmoil
is in the country because of the wretch you put to death?"

I thought to check her tongue but there was no use in
that, Rhesa. I was unable to stir. There was some witchery

in her venomous eyes which held me there while the
people were coming to surround me from every direction.

"And the Emperor will summon you to Rome and your
sovreignty will be taken from you and you will be banished to a foreign country and a multiplicity of diseases
and maladies will strike you. . . . In a vision I see a rotten
filthy old man lying on mountain sedge in a hovel and
hundreds of thousands of maggots squirming into his
flesh and burrowing into his bones. He has long grey hair
and a handful of it comes away every time he scratches
himself. There is nobody to care for him. What goes in
his mouth as food comes out as great oaths. . . ."

She burst out laughing.

"And you think you will have peace when I am not
near you! Don't think it, fool! I will be near you. I will!
I will! But being there, I shall have only this concern, to
remind you time to time that it is because of the woman
you once loved you are in such a condition. . . ."

She died a month ago, Rhesa. She never left me but
tormented me from dawn to dusk. I am astonished,
Rhesa, foster-son, at the hatred and jealousy of betrayed
women. Yet I am far more astonished at the species of
philosophy to be had at present in Rome; sit here near
me and tell me a little more about the philosophy of the
Stoics about which you spoke before. . . .but take care
against the maggots; they are around you everywhere. . . .

Music and Memory

translated by Niall Toibin

I

Last night in bed, what I saw was....

A tiny room, bare but for two chairs, a table standing under a broken window, a low bed fit only for a child or someone of no great height. There was an old man in the room, the signs of sorrow plain to be seen on his noble face. He wore cord breeches, heavy cobbler's boots crusted with the mud of the streets, a shawl over his shoulders. He had long grey hair, his head was bowed, and he sat quite still on the floor beside the low bed. I saw him only by the fire-light, for the small tin lamp hung unlit on the white-washed wall.

The door banged. Two people came in. The old man didn't raise his head. He didn't speak. The pair who had entered — a stooped old woman and a girl who looked no more than seventeen — spoke no word either. They seemed not to see the sad old man at all, yet it was he who held my own attention as I tried to imagine what could have brought so great a sorrow on him.

The woman and the girl moved slowly across the floor. I could see that the girl was leading the old woman. They made for the low bed. As she got to the bed the old woman reached out a worn brown hand. It came to rest on the brow of a young woman who lay there. Was it asleep she was, the young woman? That was my first thought, till the old woman took to wailing and they both fell to their knees and began feverishly to pray for the dead.

But the sad old man neither spoke nor moved. He just sat on the floor, his head bowed.

The girl rose. In her hands she held flowers and she shook a spray of them over the corpse. Neither of the others paid any heed to her or to what she was about, and I found that strange.

"I get the smell of honeysuckle," said the old man, after a while. "If my daughter were alive...."

"'Leave a spray of honeysuckle in the coffin', that's what she said yesterday," said the girl. "I left town in the early morning to pluck it...." And she wept bitterly.

Suddenly the old man got up. Across the floor he paced, then back again. He was very agitated. Not from sadness, not from sorrow but from greed. Greed and greed alone is what shows in his face as he bends over the bed, showering the corpse with kisses. Terrifying greed in his look....

"I'd give up my share of Heaven, my share of God's Heaven, to see you my treasure, to see you my love.... to have the sight of my eyes for one moment, one short moment, one little moment Almighty God of Glory! All I want on this earth is to see my darling child before they put her in the clay. Oh God, oh God of Glory hear my prayer."

*

Last night in bed what I heard was....

The melody that moved my heart, music sweet, subdued and pleasing, a lullaby to soothe a madman.

As I opened my eyes I beheld the old sad man who had sat on the floor beside the deathbed, holding a violin. The music he played was no melodic trickle, no cascade of sweetness or swell of sound, but the room seemed filled with music, as though the performer's art made audible miraculous sounds which the human ear could never else have heard till the end of time.

The whisper of waves on the seashore of a quiet summer's day was in that music; what that music called to mind were gardens of great swaying blooms where stately ladies strolled in contentment. One felt like sleeping, like falling sound asleep forever, but there was no taking one's eyes off the tranquil face of the player.

The lullaby continued. To my own ear the snore of a child came through the music, which grew softer and softer till in the end I could hear only the snoring. But I knew by the player that he could still hear the soothing tune. It seemed forever in his ears.

Have you no thought, blind fiddler, for your child, your daughter stretched cold and dead so near you?

*

Last night in bed what I heard was....

Joyous merry music from the same musician, music to set your feet a-dancing, music to lift the sorrow from your heart. But the real magic of that music was that as one listened, it evoked a myriad sights that came and went with changes in the tune. I saw in the distance a wide plain. Trees here and there bent with the breeze. Many-coloured flowers. Soft white clouds chased one another across the skies and I heard, yes I heard, the same merry music come to me on the wind. But as I cocked an ear the better to hear it, I heard not a sound. The music faded away, but the view remained of that beautiful plain, and in the heart of the plain I saw two people, an old man and a little girl. He played while she danced, danced light-heartedly, her long hair flowing in the wind.

But when I raised my head again, all I saw was the old man squatting on the floor holding his fiddle, not with his old expression of sadness but with the serene face of that player on that pleasant plain. Shame on you, old man, to be merry and your daughter dead.

The music changed once more and I saw a roadway, long, cold and wet. An old man and a young girl walked that road. Both worn out and weary. He cantankerous. She grasping his hand, leading him, trying to placate him, telling him they had not long more to go, that they would be home within the hour, by a warm fire with food and comfort, that all would soon be as it should....

Child, child, what makes you tell such lies?

Pay no heed to her old man, old blind fiddler squatting on the floor, don't believe one word. If you were not blind, isn't it well you'd recognise that it was on that same long, wet, cold road she met that wretched thief, that cursed thief who stole her from you....? To think of a father music-making and his daughter dead!

*

In bed last night what I heard was....

The most doleful music I've heard in all my life. It held the mourning of a father and the mourning of a mother, the mourning of a friend for a friend, the mourning of a lover for his beloved. I covered my ears because that music went right through me, through the core of my being. I wanted to rise and leave but I couldn't, the old music-man wouldn't let me stir. He kept a tight grip of me. He seemed set to tear my heart in two and might have, but that an abrupt stop was put to the music.

A pair came into the room the player was in, a stooped old hag being led by a young girl. The old woman was blazing with anger.

"We've been listening to you this half-hour," said the old woman. "Fitter for you to be on your two knees beside that bed than making music and your daughter dead...."

The old man said nothing. He never moved. The violin lay on the floor beside him, gripped in his left hand. His right hand was flung across the low bed, his head nestled on his daughter's corpse.

When the old woman failed to get any good of him or coax any speech from him, they left, the old woman shouting how she'd let the neighbours know how little he grieved for his daughter. But as he began to play again, after they had gone, I understood. It came to me that it was no music he was playing, but putting himself in mind again of the life that he and his daughter shared while she lived.... and the life he himself would have after her death.

It's not pity I feel for you, old man, old blind musician, when I know what a rare jewel is yours to bestow on your daughter who is dead....

II

A letter that came yesterday told me my old friend the music-man had passed away.

My poor blind fiddler. The news plunged me into morose recollection of the old days and of the way I first met him.

We were both adrift, wandering rudderless over the world in those days; I a soft young lad, without home or house or hope, down to my last sixpenny piece; he a tough tormented old man, busking tunes for graceless strangers in a big city far from home. Both without home or house or hope — just a single sixpence between the pair of us.

A wet night in a foreign town. My feet in tattered shoes that squelched with the wet. Heavy of heart, any love I

owed my own or any of mankind scoured clean away.
Oh! That night!

But I heard the music. The soft, kindly Irish music.
And I watched the player, who stood in a pub door to
catch the stray pennies of the stranger. I liked the cut of
him, an old beret pushed well back on his head, he stood
clasping his fiddle, his aristocratic face shining in the
light of the pub window.

But it was that soft, sweet Irish air he played that held
me there on the kerb till the music stopped. And when it
did, I did an odd thing, a foolish thing if you like.

This was what I did.

I took the last, solitary, shining sixpence I had in this
world, tossed it into the music-man's collection box and
hurried off. I hadn't gone twenty yards before regret
overtook me. I began to brood over all that that fine
sixpence might have bought me. A loaf of bread, a hunk
of cheese, a glass of bitter.... Every baker's shop I passed,
I stared in the window at the fine loaves of brown bread,
the tempting sweet cakes. Every ale-house I saw annoyed
me more as the smell of the drinks I couldn't have came
at me through the door.

I was sick that I had parted with that sixpence.

I went back. The blind player was fiddling away outside another pub door. I saw my own bright sixpence on
its own among the red pennies on the floor of the
collection-box. What remorse I felt. My heart was full.
My belly was empty. I began to vent my resentment in
a curious kind of outburst such as one rarely hears
through life. I spoke in Irish lest the gentle, blind musician
should suspect my black spite against the world, or the
vicious spleen that lurked within me. And it wasn't the
thought of that last sixpence that maddened me. No, it
was....

Anyway, I bared my soul to that blind man in a city

over the sea, sure that he understood not a word of what I said.

But he did. He understood all I said. What was more, he realised what heartbreak had prompted me to speak.

"My poor man!"

His words took me aback, filled me with shame for what I had said.

"My poor, poor man," he said again, in a voice filled with strange compassion.

"So you speak Irish?" I said. "If I had known that I'd never have made such a confession before you."

He said nothing. He just took hold of my hand and I sensed affection, sympathy and insight in that blind man's touch.

We moved on, I leading him. Picture us, an old blind man carrying a fiddle with a stick in his left hand, white-faced, noble, with no sight of the pallid youngster by his side, of the grimy streets or the brightly-lit shops or the viciousness, greed and meanness in the faces of the passers-by.

"I envy you, blind man, that you can't see the squalor of the world," I said, in my own mind, as I thought, but perhaps I spoke aloud, for the old man answered me, if answer it was.

His voice was low and soft, as is with the blind.

"God granted me gifts untold, my foolish lad," he said, "and He'll grant the same to you, if you accept them."

A cold wet night in a foreign town, the squelch of water in my worn-out shoes, the drone of hunger in my belly, evil in my heart, the serene philosophy of a blind man in my unheeding ears....

"God is good. He never stops speaking to anyone with ears to hear Him...."

The old man went on talking and I felt I had never heard such uplifting words from the mouth of man.

"You only need to listen to Him," he said, "and He will fill your poor black soul with joy. I was one time...."

But he said no more, and when he asked me to go with him to his little room, I gratefully agreed.

We climbed five or six flights of stairs to the top of a tall lodging house and entered a room bearing all the marks of poverty. But for all its meagreness and bareness it contained a hint of refinement, not the air of a solitary occupant.

In the middle of the floor a rickety old table covered with a cloth, two chairs of different makes, a three-legged stool no carpenter ever made, a small shelf on the wall with a few utensils, a little bed in the corner. This was all one noticed at first. But where you find flowers, you find woman. And this poor room held flowers, or rather buds, since it was still early spring. They were all over the room, buds of thorn bush, of the golden furze even, however the like was come by in the centre of a huge city. Six or seven pictures were pinned to the walls. Only a woman would have picked those pictures, given the choice.

But where was the woman?

The fire in the grate was well-night out and the old man on his knees trying to blow it back to life. A little flame would flicker from the embers, he would heap some twigs on it, it would flare so that you saw clearly the pale brow of the blind man, the long, slim musician's fingers and the big, blue veins standing out on the back of his hands, like the stripped twigs of a tree against the frosty sky of a winter's evening.

I thought to help him, but he wouldn't have it. I was forced to sit there watching him and listening to the ferocity of the elements. And what music they made. The house we were in was the highest in the street, and the gales lashed round the roof and roared down the chimney and under the door, and as the rain whipped against the windows, one might have been in a prison with packs of wild animals outside howling for blood.

The old man stayed on his hunkers over the fire, while I sat on the stool splitting wood. He raised himself a little and gripped my knee.

"God protect us," he said, "but we're better off here tonight as bad as 'tis, than out in a fishing smack under Gulam Head."

"And do you tell me you were out there?" I asked in astonishment, for at that time, of course, I didn't know where he was from, but the very mention of that place had made my heart leap. I saw before my eyes the Head itself, the sea about it, the Aran Islands. I sighed.

The old man didn't answer my question. He was tending a can of milk over the fire and talking to himself, heedless of me. "Gulam Head," he would say, and from the slow, easy way he spoke each word it was plain that he saw all the places clearly before his two blind eyes. I myself could see them in any case.

"Gulam Head, and a decent boat to go hunting seals .... little white sheep on the fisherman's plain.... the fish gobbling.... you'd no sooner drop a line than you had a bite.... haul it in.... throw it there on the bottom.... and out she goes again...."

He certainly didn't suspect that I had ever been to the place or had any hand in the sport of the sea-fisherman, for he asked me no question about it. He simply handed me a cup of the hot milk, and I promise you I needed it that fearsome night.

Before long I was more at ease. I felt a fine warmth from the milk surge through my veins and the fire revived my limbs. I no longer worried about rain or storm. The gales that screeched around that gloomy old lodging-house, like a thousand wild beasts, bothered me not the least....

After I'd had a bite to eat I was feeling satisfied and snug.

It took a while for me to convince the old man that I had as good a knowledge of Gulam Head as he had. By then he was over the fire eating his supper and paying no attention to me. But he was there only in the flesh.... in his mind he was ploughing the ocean and splitting the waves, battling storm and gale on the wide and fickle sea.

Choppy seas and raging swells, menacing rocks and towering cliffs were all he saw with his blind eyes as he crouched over the fire in a barren room in an alien city....

I wanted to talk to him, to tell him how much I loved these things of which he'd spoken. I wished I could coax more lore from him, question him closer about the gifts that God had given him, for what he had told me on the street before we came in had begun to press on my mind by now, yet I hated to trespass on his happy reverie or probe his secret life.

"Gulam Head," he would say, "Gulam Head.... Cuan an Fhir Mhoir.... Dangan.... Kilkieran Bay...." And I couldn't help but see every single place as if I were there.

Footsteps sounded outside the door. The old man started. He put aside the dreams of his youth. A young woman came in.

"This is my daughter," he said.

I was held in a trance by the loveliness of the girl.

I don't believe I have ever had a stranger meal than the one I shared that night with the blind musician and his daughter in that small bare room in a city so far from home.

My appetite was good, but I ate little. Indeed, I rose from that table as hungry almost as I had sat down to it, and not for want of food, but because of that girl, the old man's lovely child....

She had startled me when first she came into the room. I had not expected such a woman, so eerily graceful, so gracefully eerie.... she had blushed a little, perhaps because of the way I watched her, or perhaps from the exertion of climbing the stairs.

"Rosie," her father said, "this man is another poor exile."

She acknowledged me. No queen could have done so with more majesty.

Her father told her how we had met. "And you won't delay, will you," he said, "getting a meal for us. The hunger is gnawing the pair of us."

"The three of us," she said.

There isn't a word she spoke that night that I cannot recall tonight. I remember how she spoke it and every gesture she made as she conversed. I need but close my eyes to see her.... her face a mite too thin and pale maybe, and the blush that came and went whenever I looked too long at her. Her black hair, untamed as her own spirit .... but no phrase can convey that eerie grace, that graceful eeriness of which I spoke before. The beauty, the mystery lay not in her looks or her speech alone, but in the fusion of all....

*

During the meal the old man spoke once more.

"Rosie," he said, "I was imagining just now that I was back home again in Connemara.... out boating I was.... ploughing the ocean and splitting the waves.... out on the deep on my own in the little *pucan*.... and I had the eyes of this world again...."

From time to time he put a stop to his speech, as

though he hoped to be interrupted. But neither of us bothered much with him. For myself I heard very little of what he said. If I got Ireland free and full of cattle, I couldn't pay due heed to him, for my eyes were fastened on the girl.... I made an effort not to stare, but I might have been reaching for the moon. I no sooner turned an eye and an ear to the old man, than I'd feel myself straining to catch the most casual word she let slip.

And her confusion was just as plain. She put salt in her father's tea and passed me the milk when asked for bread; when the blind man told her to fill the kettle, she got up and opened the door, and then she laughed, though she didn't know why.

I felt pity for her and pity for myself. Once again I made myself listen to the awful howling of the wind, to the rain pelting against the window, to the raucous wrangling of the lodgers downstairs, but it was no good. I had eyes and ears and interest for nothing but for her.

"If you're finished, we'll sit up to the fire," said the old man.

I hadn't eaten enough, nor half enough, but we did as he suggested. I chose a seat where she couldn't see my face. She sat on a small stool and flung a friendly hand across her father's knee.

"I was telling you while ago," he said, "that I could see all with eyes of this world."

"Could you, father?"

"Yes. I saw Gulam Head rising up from the sea. I sailed east on Kilkieran Bay and I saw the little village with the white houses and Modhardan Hill above beyond it."

"Wouldn't I love to be there," she sighed, and she started to remember many places I knew as well. She spoke eloquently, pleasantly, but I noticed that she spoke with odd inaccuracy about the local people. She talked of some who were dead before she was born as if they still lived. It gave great weirdness to her talk, a woman of little more than twenty, reminiscing about old times like a granny.

She spoke highly or belittlingly about folk who were in their graves when I was a wee lad, in a way that would make you shudder.

"And when did you last see these people and places?" I asked her.

"Never," said she, "but my father talks so much about them I know some of them better than I know anyone hereabouts."

Then I partly understood that eeriness of hers, when she could say that she had never seen Ireland, but knew people well who had lived there in her father's boyhood.

I think now she may have done it to tease me, but she described the bad habits of a tailor who was still alive when I was a child.

"But he's dead this twenty years!" I said. "So what great age are you?"

"Oh, I'm as old as my father! Isn't that right, dad?" And she got up and started to sing like a lark.

A strange woman.... a strange man.... a strange trio we made together in that sparse, bare top room of a lodging house in an alien city far from home.

*

You might think a novice in matters of love could guess the end of my tale with no help from me. A misguided youth careering downhill to rack and ruin, who falls in love with a busker's daughter.... that's all there is to that. So you might say. But wait!

The first night I met her, that night her father invited

me home to eat in their bare room, I knew that night
already that our two hearts beat as one.

And thought we had not the same rearing nor the same
kind of life up to then, I knew God meant her for me from
the dawn of Time. Don't ask me what kind of woman she
was. It's hardship enough here alone on this hillside to
think about her, never mind explain her to the world. But
I ask any man who reads this to close his eyes and think
for five minutes of the Deirdre of his own heart, so that
he may have a truer picture of this woman who stole my
heart and mind.

That springtime! It will stay with me through eternity.
I was stripped of the rags of care and distress. I was
young, the world was young, and the beauty and freshness
and fragrance of the world had robbed me of all sense
.... or given me back all my sense, it might be more true
to say.

No work? No money? No pleasure that is the due of
youth? That soured me not one whit. If I arose to face no
breakfast, what matter? Hadn't I a fine strong leather
belt to tighten round my middle? And an extra notch to
pull it tighter come dinner time? But no words can
describe the elation with which I waited for nightfall
when I could converse with my sweet, mysterious Rosie.

It's not that I mooned about her night and day in the
way of the poets with their ladies. It wasn't like that at
all, but that I felt she was thinking of me always, that she
knew in some unexplainable way what I was doing from
dawn till dusk. Not everyone knows of that secret bond
between true lovers. I cannot fathom it rightly myself but
I know that such a bond exists. One way or another it
kept me from harm. God knows what other sins might
weigh down my soul but for it.

How ashamed I felt when I did something that I dared
not tell her. I was often mortified like that and once or

twice I skipped my usual visit to her house. I could not bear to sit there in her presence with any bad thing on my conscience. You could only liken it to taking Communion in the state of mortal sin.

But don't think that she was inquisitive. No. She never pried nor questioned nor badgered in all the time I knew her. Her own heart and soul were bright and sinless and she had no thought that her friends could be otherwise.

Whenever some secret guilt kept me from her I carried my own black hell within my heart. But if true contrition scrubs the soul of sin, then many and many a time my own soul must have shone. I recall one such night. My heart was black as coal and I had resolved to clear out of the country and never to see her again.

To desert my sweet, mysterious Rosie. My heart was bursting asunder as I set out to pay my last visit to her.

Would I be man enough to tell her the truth, to confess and then go to the devil, for where else could I wind up without her at my side to help me?

She was alone when I called in.

I thought her eyes seemed brighter, her cheeks more flushed than usual. Could she tell by me, in some strange way, that I had done something ugly and shameful?

"Rosie," I said, "I must leave this country tomorrow."

She didn't speak. She was too upset. My words had wounded her too deeply. "And we'll never see each other again," I said, and I plucked up the courage to tell her my whole sordid story.

I neither put to it nor took from it. Looking back I'm sure I told the honest truth.

She said no word till I had done. What I thought then was that she would surely order me out of the house never to return. That, in any case, was what I deserved.

I sat gazing into the fire, humiliated. It seemed an age before she spoke. I couldn't bear to look at her, not for

Ireland free; but I felt her gentle hand lightly caress my head, her hair brushed against my cheek, sending what might have been an electric charge through my body, and I rose and took her in my arms, and kissed her passionately on the mouth, the first and only time I kissed my sweet mysterious Rosie.

*

And ten calamitous years went by before I spoke to her again. I'd been back and forth about the world in-between times and mostly in no mood to write to anybody and all I got from Rosie was two letters in the first year, because I was moving about so much.

But as soon as we touched the quayside in the port where she was living, I made up my mind to pay her a visit, though I had sworn twice a day throughout that voyage never to trouble her again.

I knew nothing of how things stood, whether she had married or not. Had she grown to the beauty that was the promise of her youth? Had time taken her down a peg, softened the "Who-but-me" in her? How headstrong she could be when I'd known her first. I remembered the glint in her eye if she was crossed. She was ever her own woman. The control she held over me although I was — I won't say how many years — older than she was.... The restraint she could impose was what had softened me.

Restraining, yet generous, she could set my heart singing, like a ray of early morning sunshine.

I wondered as I headed for the house what she was like now. Twenty-six.... when woman is most womanly. Her merry green eyes at least would still be the same; neither age nor eternity could quench their sparkle or laughter. Black, black hair.... too unkempt maybe, but I only found the courage to tell her so once.... long features, a shade too pale.... but her soft, soft fragrant skin! I remembered one morning burying my face in apple-blossoms.... they smelt no sweeter than that skin of hers.

I regretted not having written to her over the long years. How did I know she would still be there at all?

A lump rose in my throat as I knocked at the door of that tall lodging house where first I had met her. I felt at least a hundred years go by before I got an answer.

A slatternly woman I didn't recognise opened the door. I asked for my Rosie, my heart in my mouth.

"She's a bit better today," said the woman. "She drank some milk and managed to eat an egg."

What was wrong with her? I hesitated, afraid to ask. But I was eaten with anxiety. It was hard to credit how agitated I had become because this girl I had not seen for ten years was sick. I was shown into the room where she lay. A shock of horror ran through me at the sight of her. She looked like death.... the twinkling eyes were closed .... no colour showed in her face but white. One hand was outside the bedclothes, a long slim hand, sinews and veins showing through the wax-white flesh.

I sobbed. This was the woman I'd known so hale and headstrong ten years before. The woman who had kept her hold on my heart wherever I went.

She opened her eyes with a start. Some colour came back to her cheek when she saw me. Each of us read the look that came into the other's eyes, and we both understood.

What did we not have to tell each other, neither knowing where to begin. Each of us knowing full well what had bound us in the past, and each of us knowing for certain that not even time, ill-health nor all the evil of my life had snapped the bond. Old memories flooded in on us, coming and going with the speed of lightning. The old life we had shared was still ruling our thought, but all that had intervened — her sickness and my own debauchery — sought to assert themselves above the memory of that life.

We stayed silent for a long while, but some mystic current of truth flowed from one to the other, so that I comprehended what she had gone through in the ten years, and the young woman perceived the evil that I had done throughout that time. And this mystic truth was more pure and precise than anything either of us could have conveyed by word of mouth.

When we did speak, we conspired to hide this mystic truth from each other, but we failed. Our eyes told what our words concealed, and some sense of shame compelled us to know each other better through silence than by any other means.

She knew that often and often I had thought about her but wouldn't let on to myself. And I knew that nothing had scalded her own heart more than the fear that she might die without ever seeing me again, but that she wouldn't let on to me or to herself.

"There was one day," she said, "and you were about to commit a horrible crime.... That same day...."

But I won't tell what she said, or what I said. She is in her grave this month and her soul is in Heaven. Seeing that she saved me from dreadful wrong while she lived and breathed, can she not do so even more now that she is with God?

Say a prayer for her soul; her like I'll never meet again in this valley of tears.

Paidin Mhaire

translated by Con Houlihan

I

It is now nine years since Baile-an-Churrigh was in a
ferment owing to the public works that had been started
to assist the poor.

A road was being made from Oilean-na-Tra to Caladh
Eamainn — and a fair amount should be done between
the tides before the result of the labour could be seen
above the water. But if a gang striving might and main
could alter the face of the shore, then these were the men
for the job. They were toiling diligently among the rocks,
battling against the tides that came rapidly and held up
the work until they ebbed. You could hear the smiting of
their sledges and the ringing of their hammers near and
far as they struck sparks from the rocks they were drilling
so that they could put in the powder and blow them
asunder.

It was a great sight to watch them matching their
strength and their ingenuity against that wild shore.
There were hundreds of them, young and old, working in
little teams of three — and their veins and their sinews
swelled and contracted with every blow.

"We're deep enough now," shouted the man who was
holding the drilling-bar for Paidin Mhaire and Stiofan
Pheig.

The pair threw down their sledges and started to clean out the hole they had drilled.

"Upon my soul," said Paidin, "this is heavy work. I'd far rather be out in the pookawn with Sean Beag under Gulam Head. With this kind of wind 'twould be a great day for catching wrasse."

"Bad cess to them for wrasse," said the man with the drilling-bar. "Who would bother looking for them while he had the public works? You'd spend long days after them before they'd bring you in seven shillings and sixpence a week."

"You'd make it in one day if you met a shoal," said Paidin as he impatiently packed the powder into the hole.

"Let them to those that couldn't get work here this morning — I wouldn't throw away a safe job to go after them," said Stiofan as he wiped the sweat from his brow with the sleeve of his gansey.

But Paidin wasn't convinced at all. He was a fisherman — and since childhood had spent only rare days on land until this bad year came. Now he had to go on the public works to support his parents who were no longer robust. And he was inclined to be restless when he wasn't in a boat. He was one of the Connolly clan — and 'twas said of them that they were kin to the seals. And you could well believe it — because whenever a raincloud came in across the sea it affected him with sadness. And when the spring tide came he used to feel a corresponding surge in his blood that compelled him to go out on the water.

"You've enough done," said one of his comrades to Paidin as he packed the powder tighter into the hole. "The job is right now. Light the fuse."

The other man went off to warn the rest. Paidin lit the fuse that went down to the powder in the hole. Then he and the others nearby took cover.

They waited a few minutes for the explosion. Nothing happened. They waited a few more minutes restlessly.

Then they waited a full five minutes more until their patience gave out.

" 'Tis how it failed," said one of the company.

"Maybe it didn't — 'tis better have patience," said another.

They waited until they again lost patience.

Then the ganger said: "It failed — we must clean out the hole."

Then the rest went off in little gangs of three to bend their backs as they drilled again — while Paidin and his two comrades went to clean out the hole. They walked around the rock cautiously at first but as nothing happened they got bolder and came nearer to it.

And then it blew — the rock went sky-high in fragments and the air was darkened with sand and gravel and smoke and there was the smell of powder.

The men threw down their implements and made off as fast as they could to the shelter of the rocks.

But Paidin lay stretched, his face riddled with sand and one eye ruined. The doctor came and did all he could — but declared that he couldn't be sure if he would recover or die.

The unfortunate man was placed in a boat and taken to his little mud house near Caladh Eamainn where his parents were waiting for him.

"What a pity, Paidin, that 'tisn't out fishing you were to-day — the place that's natural for you is the best place for you," said Stiofan as he left the house.

Paidin lay stretched on his soft bed with his mother for nurse.

II

Paidin was a great lively powerful man who had hardly ever known sickness in his life and within a month he was fairly well. But the sight of one eye was gone forever and the other eye was affected too. He got £50 compensation from the Public Works authorities — and felt that himself and his parents would never see a poor day again.

He bought a rowing boat and made a mast and sails for it; he got nets and hooks and went back fishing. But the trouble was that if ever he happened to meet a neighbour, he couldn't let him go without buying him a drink. And indeed it often happened that three or four would walk in while he was in the pub and he wouldn't be happy if he didn't ask them all to have a drink. And then sometimes after a few glasses they would insist on buying their round too — and then at closing time they'd all go off to some house where there was card-playing and music and dancing and poteen. Paidin loved the poteen and the music and the card-playing. He was in the flower of youth and the blood was pulsing in his veins. And now that he had money after having been for so long pulling the devil by the tail he abandoned all restraint and he had his fling.

And of course all this carry-on ate away at his money. Within a year he hadn't much left and when the summer came again all his compensation was gone down the drain. He was trying to survive by the fishing until the potatoes were ready for digging — and hardly succeeding.

Paidin and his parents were now in a bad way. His good eye was failing — and he couldn't do much work. He used to talk to himself as he sat on a rock on the shore and looked into his conscience: "Wasn't I the reckless fellow that brought this misfortune on my parents in the latter-end of their days. . . ." Then the hot blood would surge again — and he would be as tempted to go on a carouse as when he had the money.

He used to go out fishing on his own — but he couldn't go very far on account of his sight. He used to stay out on the water until the sun went down — and the ripples and the waves and everything bound up with the sea brought

a kind of peace to his soul. But, indeed, that was often all
he got — and on the way home he'd be examining his life
again.

And the time came when he was getting so little from
the fishing that his parents were destitute — and so
Paidin went to the Relieving Officer and sought assistance
from them.

"Have they anything at all to support them?" asked
the official.

"Nothing whatever," said Paidin.

"And who was supporting them until now?"

"I was," said Paidin, "but for a good while now I
amn't able."

"Well, if that's the case," said the officer, "the only
place they can get assistance is in the Poorhouse."

"And why is that?" said Paidin as the anger smote
him.

"Because," said the officer, "you are not in the Poorhouse. There are only two things you can do: either they
will go in — or else you will go in and they can stay
outside and get Assistance."

He spoke as if he were reading out of a book — and
Paidin went home very angry. He knew now that he
would have to go to the Poorhouse. He couldn't let his
parents go in there — and he wasn't able to support
them.

He walked home across the lonesome marshland that
lies between Caladh Eamainn and Coill Mhairtin. He
was walking by the brink of the sea and listening to the
restless voice of the tide and his whole body was aching
with the shame that afflicted him as he thought of how he
had squandered his money. He knew that his good eye
was getting worse and worse. He looked out west over
Chuan Casla — but couldn't see the island of Aran even
though it was a fine summer day and the thrush was
singing blithely from a furze-bush nearby. He had often

heard that anyone with fairly good sight could see Aran any day that the thrush was down in that marsh. He knew now that he was going blind entirely. He closed his good eye to try and feel how it was to have no sight. He tried to walk but felt himself going hither and thither. He tried to correct himself — but only succeeded in falling into a bog-hole.

"Oh Lord God," he said out loud. "Have pity on me and don't take away my sight. Please, Lord, please don't."

He went in home to his mother.

"What news have you?" said she.

"Bad news then," he answered.

"God between us and all harm. But tell it to me anyway."

"I'll be in the Poorhouse before the summer is over and I'll be blind before Christmas — but ye'll get Public Assistance here at home."

"God between us and misfortune — you have no need at all to go into that place," said his mother.

"I must, Mam," said Paidin, "because if I remain outside, ye'll be entitled to nothing. That's their law — and my curse on it for a law. But what hurts me most of all is that I have to humiliate myself before them for your sake."

The old woman began to cry and to rave and to say that she would take to the bed.

"Give over the lamenting, mother," said Paidin. " 'Twas I spent the money — and I'll suffer for it."

She couldn't persuade Paidin that day — and then she used to say to him that maybe his eye would improve in the hospital and that he would come home to them with good sight.

But it didn't happen that way. He was barely inside before he was totally blind.

III

It was a bright autumn day and the inmates of the Poorhouse were happy sunning themselves when they saw a man coming towards them, feeling his way with a stick.

And said one of them: " 'Tis the wild boatman from Caladh Eamainn."

"It is indeed," said another.

The first man spoke again: "Since he came in here his sight is gone — and unless I'm mistaken his sense is nearly gone too: he fights with the Master and everyone else."

"Before he's long more here he'll be taught sense," said a bleary-eyed little man who had been there for seven years.

"Do ye know what he did this morning?" said an old man who had only one hand.

They all said that they hadn't heard a word about it.

"Well, 'twas like this. He put the handle of a brush into a crevice in the wall and broke it and said 'I'll get another tiller out of this, Sean — indeed I will.' They'll make him toe the line, I'm telling ye. . ."

"Ah the poor man," said another old fellow, who was bent and had the signs of the sea on his face. "He was never used to being confined."

The debate dwindled away because Paidin was now nearing them, walking steadily and carefully with his stick in front of him.

"You're on the right track," said the old man with the sea in his face, "keep coming."

Paidin sat down on the bench near him and raised his head, hoping to see the sun. Some of the others went away to get a few shreds of tobacco from someone who had a few ounces. The old man with the sea in his face stayed with Paidin.

And Paidin said to him: "The sun is direct from the south — and unless I'm very much mistaken the wind is from the south-west."

"Right," said the old fellow, " 'tis hard to beat a boatman when it comes to the wind."

"There's a spring tide rising," said Paidin.

" 'Tis full tide at Beal an Chuain," said the old man.

"You were a boatman too?" said Paidin.

" 'Tis full tide at Beal an Chuain — and 'tis starting to ebb under Gulam Head," said the old man.

"If that's how 'tis, we won't get to the Quay at Ross in this tide."

"If we won't, she isn't much of a boat. Tidy up the sail and I'll throw out some of the ballast."

Paidin began to draw into him the rope he had by his side and he kept his back against the blackthorn stick he had wedged into a crevice in the wall. The old man was throwing away the stones that were around him.

"She's in a hurry now if ever she was. Look at the white flowers she's leaving behind her. I always knew that she could sail as well as any other boat. Is that Marcus Mor's boat that's trying to come between her and the wind?" said Paidin — and he pretended to be watching another boat keenly.

"It is — but the rock at Beal an Chuain will thwart her," said the old man as he lay on his belly with his eyes narrowed like a boatman on the look-out.

"Is that a seal out in front of us?" said Paidin.

"It is surely," said the old man. "If only I had my gun. . ."

"Why?" said Paidin.

"To fire at him, of course."

Paidin threw the rope away. He shifted from the imaginary helm and made the Sign of the Cross.

"The Lord save us and guard us," said he. "You would

do such a thing — and one of the Connolly tribe in the boat with you?"

"I would," said the old man. "And I wouldn't care who was with me."

"If you did," said Paidin fiercely, "I'd lay into you with this stick until your last drop of blood was spilt."

Then a man spoke behind Paidin: "Look there now, you savage — don't hit a greyhaired old man."

He was one of a little crowd who had been watching for a while in great wonderment.

Then the bell rang and the other inmates began to arrive. Paidin said to the old man that every one of the Connollys had to protect the seals because they were their cousins. He couldn't say any more because the steward was ordering silence.

And so one after another the inmates went through the big door without a word or a laugh — some of them indeed without as much as a thought.

IV

They were an orderly lot as they entered the room set out for them, some of them looking longingly at the teapots, and others at the bread that was at the top of every table. And there were some who were getting the last out of the little pieces of tobacco they were chewing in a way that the steward wouldn't see them.

Paidin was the last to sit down. Every evening he would sit in the same place drinking his tea out of the same cup — and with the same people around him. That was the way it had been every night since he came — but now he was in a restless irritable mood. The noise all around made him sullen. He imagined that they were all looking at him — and hostile towards him. He thought that every morsel he put in his mouth was being watched by a score of people. He listened for a while to their voices. He tried to imagine it was the sound of rowing — but he didn't succeed. Then he heard the singing of the river that flowed by the house on its way to the sea telling him a story. Then he cocked his ear in an attempt to get some meaning out of the noise that was deafening him. He thought he did — and shouted "Stay where you are — stay where you are."

A laugh came from those around him. And he jumped up in a great fit of anger because he thought they were making fun of him.

"Ye scum of the earth," he said. "Is it at me ye're laughing? Don't forget that I'm more than a match for anyone of ye." And he waved his stick at them.

The steward came and made him sit down. He tried to drink a little tea but he wasn't able. He remained there a while restlessly — and then he took up his blackthorn and went out.

And someone said softly: "He's a wild beast that shouldn't be allowed at large."

And another said: "He's out of his mind entirely."

And the first man said: "Those who never had enough until they came here are the hardest to please."

The steward, cursing under his breath, ordered silence again. He was a miserable little fellow who had got his promotion because he used to spy on the rest. His assistant came and asked if he should go after Paidin.

"Don't bother with him," said the steward. "He won't stay out long from his supper." And so he didn't follow him.

Paidin, however, had gone out the gate as fast as ever he could with his lack of sight and got onto the road. It was a fine calm starry night. Soon he had left the Poorhouse and the surrounding village behind him. He felt himself as strong and as full of energy as ever he had been in his life. He made a leap on the road to find out if he was as agile as he had been before he went into the

Poorhouse. He felt the blood pounding marvellously in his veins — and the south-west wind coming towards him from the sea. He felt in the flower of youth once more because he was free from his term of torment. The road was disappearing behind him as he hastened along.

After a while he stopped for a little rest on a summit of the road. And he raised up his head to get the smell of the sea. It came to him. And he couldn't resist going nearer the shore — and off he went like a kid-goat on a fine spring day. But on account of his antics he went astray and found himself all alone in the bog. He was becoming tired and he didn't know which way to turn.

He shouted, hoping that someone might hear him and come to direct him. There was no one. He stood for a while — and thought he was on the bank of a river and that there was a cliff or an outcrop of rock near him. He proceeded carefully — and with his stick he found a recess under the cliff. He gathered a bundle of fern and went in to spend the night.

He lay down wearily on the ferns and began thinking. He put his head on the stones that were behind him — and soon he was asleep. In his dreams he heard the sound of the ocean near him — and the creaking of wood from boats sailing free. He was blissfully happy in his sleep.

V

A shepherd found him in the morning — he was almost dead from the cold and from the snow that had fallen heavily in the night. He was taken to a nearby house and they kept him until they discovered who he was. That didn't take long. Then he was taken to his own house.

He wasn't long there before he got a fever on account of his night in the open — and he got worse by the day. His father now even though an old man had to go back fishing to get something to add to what they were allowed by the Commissioners for the Poor.

The summer came again and the people of Baile an Churraigh and Caladh Eamainn were still pulling the devil by the tail and the men on the Public Works battling with the tides that made them break off from their labours.

You could hear the sound of their sledges and their hammers from near and far. Paidin listened as he lay at home on his soft bed.

And one day he said to his mother: "Open the door so that I can see the men working."

She did so just to please him. And he said: "Paidin Mhicil and Sean Fada are still there, mother, swinging their sledges — and unless I'm mistaken, Seanas Mhicil Mhoir is holding the bar for them."

"Without a doubt," said she. "But there's no need for you to be bothering yourself with that cursed work."

"And there's a great tide coming — just the same as the last day I was working there, look, mother, amn't I right? Do you think that if the tide came in and caught them unawares, would they be able to work under the sea? Whatever happened, the boatmen would be able to carry on their trade. Wouldn't it be a remarkable life one would have there with the whales and the seals and the porpoises as pets?"

And his mother said to him not to be talking so strangely and to rest himself.

"And, mother, aren't we related to the seals? And they'd help us under the sea because 'tis often I spoke on their behalf. Indeed they would — and we'd get a bed as soft with the sea-wrack under us — just as good as we have here. And maybe I wouldn't need sight at all there or maybe there would be a doctor among the seals that would cure me. Will you come with me, mother? And I'd see the boats over my head — and I'd recognise every one of them. I'd see them over my head as clearly as I see the two gleoiteogs now outside in Beal an Chuain.''

"Take it easy, darling — or the coughing fit will come back to you," said his mother.

The old woman put her finger near his eye but he felt nothing.

"Look," he said, "at them coming together from the Head and the workmen watching the contest. There's Marcus Beag Gleoiteog, the black one in the lead — but the other boat will get to the rock before her. Ah, Marcus, even though you are good, you aren't able to skim a limpet from a stone. There they are going around now. Upon my soul, ye rascals, ye didn't do too well — the rock at Beal an Chuain to capsize boats from the Head in that wind. . . . Alas — if I was in a boat, I'd teach ye the trade. O Marcus, Marcus, what's wrong with you that you put yourself in such danger of drowning? Help him, ye rascals, help him.''

And he sat up in his bed to go to where he thought the boats were — so that he could help the man he thought was drowning. But he couldn't get out of the bed and he was shaken by a fit. His mother was trying to put him to sleep. He tried to speak to her but he couldn't.

And then his life slipped away.

He was buried in the grave-yard south-west of Caladh Eamainn on the verge of the sea — but according to the boatmen he lies restless under the sod. On any dark dangerous night they say that he goes out on the sea helping any boatman that might be in trouble.

But it seems that his people didn't believe these stories because his mother used to be praying for him every morning at the foot of the ash-tree over his grave — until the time came for herself and her husband to go to the Poorhouse.

The Encounter

translated by John McArdle

My rowing-boat was going with the river's flow and I was lying in it without much thought for anything. It was a quiet day, seldom quieter; not a stir in the air. Sleepy amber clouds were high in the sky, busy murmuring of bees in the opening of every flower on the riverbank and the plopping lullaby of the water against my boat — little more to be heard, more to be seen, on a golden summer's day. I didn't care where the current took my boat or what calm it might stop in; I was lying in its curved palm, propped on rugs and worn coats, heedless of the living and the dead and allowing my vagrant thoughts to drift wherever will should take them. Idleness? Idleness and sleep. Sleepy idleness.

On the riverbank my hunting dog seemed as sleepy as I was. Sometimes, if he were a little ahead of the boat, he lay resting till I passed him by and when he was a little ahead again he stretched out to wait for me to catch up. Everything was tranquil and quiet, the day lengthening to evening. Summer solitude. It was hard to believe that in this world there were such things as bloodshed, drawn swords, the peal of guns, the tearing of flesh on claw or the grinding of tooth on bone. These things were far from my dog and me and the easy air of peace which hung around us.

I looked as if I was fishing for trout but it was only a pretence. The rod was in my hand all right but the fish

78

could well have been playing with my fly on the riverbed while I gazed lazily on the peaks of Mayo and The Joyce Country stabbing the sky to the north, shadows of clouds flitting across them like anger-clouds on a human brow. Fishing might be pleasant but on a day like this it was a greater thing to give thought to being alive.

I was just about to reel in the line, give up the effort of pretence and let the current be master of the boat when I noticed the transformation which had come upon my hound. I put out the oars to steady the boat in the flow. What could be the matter with him? He had come out about five yards from the bank and was standing on a pile of sandy sediment which the reeds had sifted from the stream. He was less than ten yards from me, nose sniffing, ears cocked, eyes intent. I whistled but he paid no attention to me or my whistling. Every limb was tense, every sense on edge. He was no longer the limpid companion of the riverbank but as alive and sharp as any animal I had ever seen, an arrow in a drawn bow. Suddenly it was as if the arrow were released and he thudded fast as sight into the water. The water churned and whisked along the sandy bank and by the time my eyes could make out what was happening the big red hunting-dog was scrambling around, wrestling with something in the scraggy water among the reeds.

Whatever it was was smaller than he but it struggled dreadfully. Mire and sand kicked up from the land-neck so that I could see in the thrashed water neither the hound nor the shape of his adversary. Only one could survive in such a fight. They turned and rolled and arched together; the strong wiry reeds shook and clattered against each other making a sound like the spines in the treetops of a wood tangling together in a windstorm.

The hound managed, after a long time, to wrench and drag the other animal ashore. By now it was difficult to make out his red hide, clogged as it was by the silt and sand. He had become the same colour as the spattered plunder in his stranglehold.

It was an otter. It feigned death as he hauled it in and, fooled by it, he let it fall from his grip on to the dry land. It turned quickly and made a dash on its short legs for the safety of the stream. But it wasn't quick enough and the hound pounced on it again. Gaining strength from the fierceness of its nature and the danger it was in the otter succeeded in twisting its broad low head around and sinking its teeth, short and sharp as pincers, into the hound's dark nose. Then taking advantage of the hound's momentary bewilderment, it released its grip and tried again to reach the water. But it couldn't make it. It squealed as the dog caught it by the throat and shook it venomously, the blood of the two animals mixing and blending together. He threw it into the air. He caught it again before it hit the ground. It squirmed and he jerked and shook it again till it seemed to me as I watched that both animals were on the point of exhaustion.

But the hound's strength was greater than that of the otter, his resilience like the switch-back of a sally. Suddenly he released his hold on it only to catch it again immediately. Over the heart this time. He sank his teeth in deep. Foam was coming from the mouths of the two of them, all strength teased from their limbs; you could hear their breathing in the quietness of the day; the slow racked panting of the two of them and, as the heaving of one faltered, you could hear, if your ear was sharp enough, the last pitiful weak-voiced squeak of the stream's native dweller. The kill was done.

The hound stood up on the pile of sand, thrust his nose into the air and let out a great howl of victory. It echoed through the shivering tops of the reeds and over the quiet stream, out towards where the shadows of the clouds flitted across the faces of the mountains. He was letting the world know that the ravaged being at his feet was dead and that he had done what his nature and his Maker intended he should do.

Two Brave Women

translated by Redmond O'Hanlon

It is but a short time since the following story was told to me. It is a story of an old woman whom I know and who is blind for many years. She is a widow and, so far as I am aware, had only one son.

A blind widow! From that phrase one might imagine a woman of small means. I myself thought as much when I first heard about her. But I was mistaken — badly mistaken. She was in fact a well-to-do woman. Indeed, if I had even the one-hundredth part of her wealth I could afford to spend the rest of my days in idleness.

It was about the beginning of last May that I first came to know her. I had been sent there with a message for her, but when I saw the stately residence, with servants everywhere I went and everything else in keeping, it seemed to me that I was not in the place to which I had been directed. And yet I had been instructed to visit a blind woman living among the mountains of Co. Wicklow!

When I was ushered into her room there she was before me: a slender spent old woman with pale refined features and with every inch of her proclaiming pride and haughtiness. I well remember that first sight of her. She was wearing a gown of black silk and sat in a big easy chair with her feet on a footstool. On a small table beside her lay her knitting. Motionless as a dark statue, she sat there in that great beautiful room waiting for me to speak.

"I was sent here with a message," I began.

"Yes!"

"With a message from your son...." She jerked to attention. "He told me to tell you...." I said.

But then, when I saw her anxiety on hearing her son's name, I had not the courage to deliver my message in all its bleak reality. How could I, when all I had for her was bad news? How could I tell that old blind woman that she no longer had a son; that the bones of her only child were under the sod for a month?

I decided to tell her a lie.

"Your son is alive and well over in England," I told her. "He was in the Rising, was taken prisoner and was sent overseas...."

"His name was not in the paper," the woman said. "The names of the people sent overseas were read out to me."

"He had a false name."

Lies must be fed on more lies. But what else could I do? Would you yourself be able to tell the truth to that old blind woman? How could you know the truth would not kill her if told, for instance, in this manner? "My dear lady: I pity you. You no longer have a son. I shall tell you how I first came to know him. In the middle of Dublin city a band of armed men entered a small park to occupy it as a base for the fight against the old enemy. They cleared all the people out of the park; taking it for granted that they now had the place entirely to themselves and that there was nobody left there except their own followers. They were mistaken, however. While searching the place I came on a man lying on a seat in a heavy drunken sleep. He was a middle-aged man, seemingly well-off. But from the blood smear on his forehead and the mud on his clothing it seemed he was taking a break from the country and that his way of spending his holiday was not to his own benefit. I wakened him up.

"Out of this park — and lively," I ordered.

He looked directly and truculently at me. Looking for a fight he was.

"Get out yourself," he growled.

I caught him by the shoulder.

"Here! Get a move on," I said. I didn't want to be too rough with him till he was fully awake.

But then he tried to knock me down, to trip me, and I was forced to give him a prick with the bayonet.

"May death take you," he snarled. "I have a weapon too," and before I knew what he meant he pulled a pistol from his pocket.

"Now — if you're a man," he challenged. He looked at my dress, my uniform, my belt with the ammunition, the rifle and the bayonet. He scratched his head. He rubbed his eyes. The effects of the drink were wearing off.

"And who are you yourself, if I might enquire?" he asked in some wonder.

"I am a soldier," I answered as I escorted him to the gate, "a soldier in the Army of the Republic of Ireland."

"Is it dreaming I am?" he asked. "The Republic of Ireland!"

He repeated the words three or four times as he strove to understand. If I had said that I was a Roman soldier and that Julius Caesar was my leader the poor fellow could not have been more astonished. At last he spoke.

"Tell me in confidence, young man," he said, "what date is it?"

"Easter Monday, 1916."

If one but saw him then, trying to make out what was amiss with the world! His look would have made St. Paul laugh.

I helped him to understand. "There's a rising on hand," I explained.

"A rising?"

"Yes — against the British."

He straightened himself and struck a military attitude. "Will ye take me as a soldier?"

He was completely in earnest. I did not quite know what would be the best course to take. A man is a man, and we needed men urgently. I brought him to the captain in charge.

"Have you a good shot?" he asked the man.

"As good as any man in Ireland," he answered.

"And you understand what we intend to do?"

"Very well, but I thought we never would have the chance."

And he was accepted. And he fought — fought as well as any other man who was there. During the week I came to know him very well. Both of us were together. Bombing from a housetop we were for most of the time. No man ever had a more cheerful comrade. With his stories and humour he would keep you laughing from morning to night. He had a story about a woman who had a wooden leg — there's no need to tell it here — some other time, maybe.

He was a great man for the women, though, and a great man for the drink, and yet a fighting man beyond anything else.

He never spoke to me of his mother until he was dying — yes, a bullet; a stray bullet....

It was then he told me that she was a widow; that she had no children except himself; that she was blind.

"And if you get away," he said as he was dying, "if you manage to escape you will visit her and you will tell her how I died."

I gave him my promise that I'd do so.

But when I saw that lonely blind old woman sitting there by herself in that splendid room; when I saw from the start she gave on hearing his name that she loved her son beyond telling, I lacked the courage to fulfil my promise and to tell her the truth. He who would break a woman's heart must needs be a man of courage.

*

For most of that summer I remained in the district. I was then on the run and until the pursuit was over there was no safer place. I had hardly spent two days in the neighbourhood, however, until I visited the local priest to seek his advice on the promise I had given to the man who was now beneath the clay.

The priest approved of the course I had taken.

"If you were to tell the news to her suddenly it might well be that her heart would break. The doctors say her heart is already very weak," he said.

"But," said I, "the news will have to be broken to her some time."

"I suppose so," he agreed, "but it will kill her."

As we talked a young woman came in with tea.

"Just a moment, Annie," said the priest. He introduced me to her — his sister's daughter. The priest asked me to repeat my story, which I did.

The young woman rose quickly from her chair. She spoke emphatically.

"The story of that death must be kept from her — always," she said. "To hear it would be her own death."

"But some time it will have to be told to her," said the priest.

"It need not be and it shall not be told." The girl looked at both of us. "Here!" she said "Let the three of us agree to keep the news from her while she lives."

"She will be expecting letters from him," I said.

"And she shall get them," Annie said, "for I myself will write them. Since she lost her sight it is mostly I who writes and reads letters for her while her son is absent."

There and then the three of us made a compact to withhold from the lone mother the news of her son's death.

That night the first letter was written. Annie had the pen. I was on her left; the priest on her right. For a short while no one spoke. It was as though we were afraid — composing a letter from the other world.

"My dearly beloved mother," I began, eager to get things going.

"No," said Annie, "he would not say it that way. He would only say 'mother'." She wrote down the word.

While she wrote I studied the girl closely. I saw the firmness and tension of her jaw; the shapeliness and sweep of her brows; how she moved her lips from time to time.

"My health is excellent since I left home," I put in, anxious to get ahead with the letter.

"He would not say a word about his health," said Annie and, for a moment, I thought she was about to call me a fool not to have known better the man who was dead.

"The fight in Dublin," she said and began writing, "I had a hand in that fight — you know yourself that I could never see a fight without taking part in it."

"You knew him well," I said to her.

It was the priest who spoke. "She certainly should have known him," he remarked thoughtfully.

The young woman was writing earnestly.

"I was captured in the end but I have not yet got my fill of combat and fighting."

Somehow it seemed to me a strange letter to his mother

from a son who had been captured, but the young woman was writing so authoritatively now that I was afraid to say anything. One would almost imagine that it was the dead man himself who was by her side telling her what to say.

The girl wrote much more that to me seemed ever stranger. From time to time I would glance at the priest but all he did was to sign to me to keep quiet; that she was doing fine. I was now convinced that the woman who was composing the letter knew the man who was dead better than anyone else in the world. I did not again interrupt her.

She laid the pen aside and now, with her head in her hands, she stared straight before her as though recalling some sad story from times past. The priest had thrown himself back in his chair and had his eyes closed. Very still was the room, the silence broken only by the slow heavy ticking of the clock and the breathing of the young woman wrapped in old memories. I could not keep from looking at her. Her eyes could not have held a stranger look had the dead man himself been standing there beside her, speaking to her from the world beyond in a language that no one but they themselves could understand.

I started.

". . . .and, mother dear, take good care of Annie till we meet again." It was the priest who spoke, slowly, sorrowfully.

Again the young woman took up the pen, but no sooner had she done so than she flung it from her. She began to tremble and made to rise, then burst into bitter weeping.

"Oh, Richard, Richard, Richard," she cried and hurried from the room.

I looked at the priest.

"Did she know before I told her that he was dead?" I asked.

The priest looked surprised. "I never thought of that," he said.

"Trying to hide the news from the mother. . . ." I began.

The priest interrupted me. ", ...and telling it clumsily, unfeelingly to another woman who had given the love of her heart to him," he finished.

Deeply moved, he rose to his feet.

"What a pair of fools we have been," he said.

I agreed with him.

*

Early this morning I called to the blind woman's house. Annie was there before me, reading to the old woman. To look at her now, so alive, so cheerful, you would not imagine that the girl had ever wept.

"Oh, by the way," she said, "a very nice letter came from Richard this morning."

"Read it for him," said the old lady.

We were on the lawn before the great house. The old woman sitting in an armchair taking the air, the young woman by her side in another chair. When Annie took the letter to read it to me her hands shook. She looked sharply at me. She was, I knew, trying to guess from my manner how much of her and Richard's story had been told to me. A hundred questions were in her eyes. Did I know that she and Richard were engaged to each other? Had it been told that they would have been married long ago were it not the mishap that had befallen his mother? A man who had accidentally destroyed his mother's sight with gunpowder he was drying, how could he marry a woman and care for her properly? Would it not rather be his duty to make life smooth and happy for that mother till she died?

I began to think of what the priest had said on the occasion when the young woman had hurriedly left the room. He believed that no son ever born had shown a deeper affection for his mother than had Richard for the stately old lady before me. And as for her, she was too proud, too secretive to talk about him openly or of the love she herself had for him. But if she should hear someone praising him, quietly and discreetly, as one might put it, those old wasted features would flush warmly and, ever afterwards, she would be a real friend to the speaker.

"Mother!"

The word aroused me from my meditation. Annie was quietly reading the letter of deception in a low voice, giving life and a strange emphasis to every phrase.

I can recall everything that happened that morning. I remember the place: the great chestnut tree with its fresh green leafage under which we sat; the lawn; the meadow below — within fifty yards of us a corncrake in the grass accompanied the reading of the letter with his own harsh call. But the memory most deeply engraved on my mind is the look on the face of the old woman listening closely to that spurious letter from her son, forsooth. As I looked at her I felt then that one might come to know the old woman — even know her very well — but that within her was another, a hidden life, that would never be revealed.

Annie paused in the reading.

"Read the piece he wrote about yourself, Annie," ordered the old woman.

Annie was reluctant to do so but she obeyed.

"And, mother dear, take good care of Annie."

She could read no more. Emotion overcame her. I knew she was thinking of the man to whom she had given her love and whom she would never see again.

"And I will take good care of you, Annie, till he comes to us again," the old woman promised.

I thought that Annie would break down. But she mastered her feelings though tears were in her eyes and her breathing laboured.

"Mother," she said — that was the name by which she always addressed the old woman — "I don't think it will be long until you'll see him."

What meaning the old woman took from these words I do not know. But when I looked at that dignified old lady beside me, weak, bent and alone and within — how many? — months of death, I formed my own view.

I spoke warmly then of the man who was dead. Again I told of his bravery; of his lightness of heart; of the courage he inspired in everyone near him. And as I talked the wasted wrinkled hand of the old mother stole into my own. But the gratitude of the young woman to me! The delight and pride in her eyes that the lover of her heart was thought worthy of such praise!

High in the skies a lark sang.

The old woman was moved but concerned that her emotion should not be seen.

"Off with the pair of you now," she said. "I would like to be alone for a while."

When Annie and I left for a short stroll she asked me, "Do you think she has any doubts that he is not in England?"

"I don't think she has," I answered.

"But she has a discernment that is rare," Annie persisted.

"But I'm telling you," I said, "that the manner in which you wrote that letter has deceived her."

"If she knew that her heart would break. The true story must be, must be, must be kept from her till they meet in heaven. What a weird love those two had for each other!"

By this time we were walking along the bank of a stream. Annie suddenly stopped short. Again she was staring before her and it seemed to me at first as though a whitethorn bush on the bank had drawn her attention. But it was not so. Something had deeply disturbed her.

"Oh God," she cried aloud — and in spite of herself the words slipped form her — "my heart is broken."

I asked her forgiveness for the way I had told her the story of Richard's death.

"It's not that," she said — and now she had overcome her emotion. "It is not that at all. But day and night from this time forward I must always pretend to myself that he is still active and alive; that he is writing letters to me; that soon I shall see him again."

She paused and I was about to ask her why she had to torture herself in that way.

"If I do not do so," she continued, half to herself, "some small word will some time slip from me and then the mother will understand, will know that all the time we have been deceiving her." She suddenly caught me by the shoulder.

"You must help me," she appealed.

"In what way?" I asked.

"You must pretend with me always that he is alive. My uncle must do so too."

And so it was decided. Neither Annie nor I spoke of the death of the old woman's son. Nor did the priest. Always now we turned the conversation so that anyone listening would think that the man in question was still a prisoner over in England. In a short time it was almost as if we three thought so as well.

Those two brave women!

Before much more of that summer was gone they were to give me ever further cause for wonder.

*

And what a strange summer it was to me! I had never thought I should come to know two women as I came to understand these two while I had agreed with one to deceive the other.

Often now Annie would call on me before I had finished breakfast. Some small word, perhaps, that the old woman had spoken to her had set Annie thinking until she had become half certain that the mother was now aware that we were lying to her about her son and that it was for this reason that she was failing.

How anxious Annie used to be! We would discuss these matters minutely. Earnestly we would speak of the old woman; of her small talk on hearing her son's name mentioned; of the attitudes she would strike; of the questions she would ask us when the weekly letter came. And the talk between us would last until we had succeeded in persuading each other, not only that the mother suspected nothing, but that the son was not dead at all.

From Annie's conversation you would imagine that even she herself believed that the man she had loved was still alive. Often she startled me when she would ask if I had any idea when he would come home. The unfortunate girl! There were times when in her own heart she believed the story we had concocted for the mother. And yet, was it not well for her that she found some peace of soul in that belief?

Every Friday the fictitious letter was written to the blind mother. Annie would have the pen and it was she who used to compose the greater part of the gossip. I would be by her side, adding my bit from time to time.

But indeed there was little need for this. She it was who understood the heart and mind of the man who was dead and it was seldom the apt phrase failed her. You would swear his ghost was by her side directing her pen and her thoughts.

One day she sat for a time, pen in hand. She left the pen aside and, looking before her, fell into thought. For a long while I did not interrupt her. Finally I raised my eyes and looked into hers. May I never see again such bitter sadness in the eyes of any woman.

She did not pretend to notice how I looked at her but only breathed a sigh and again took up the pen. This time she gave a detailed account of the lives of the lads in Frongoch. She wrote of the North Camp and compared it with the South Camp. She wrote too a satirical piece about the warders. In a sportive light-hearted manner she introduced some of the prisoners to the mother.

She read out the last piece she had written: "If there were a barber here," she wrote, "he would make his fortune. Either that or he would be going around, a naked madman, at the end of a week. Everyone here has a three foot beard. It is mostly music we enjoy here. . . ." She looked at me a moment and smiled; then began reading again. "This is the song most often heard here:

No blade shall reap these hairy cheeks
Till mutton chops sprout three feet long
And whiskered strength and force reveal
The man whose beard is best of all.

On the following morning this letter delighted the mother. The old worn face lit up. Annie was overjoyed.

"He is still the same, mother," she said. "Nothing in this world would upset him. In the face of death itself he would laugh and make fun."

"That is true, my dear," agreed the old woman. "There is seldom fun except where he is. The gaiety of his laughter and the lightness of his heart are a cure for ill health. For me the day is long and the night longer till I shall see him again."

Not since I had come to this place had I heard so much praise from her. The old lady was a woman of that proud stock which reveals its heart but seldom.

Annie's eyes drew me. They were dancing in her head with delight. Sweeter than honey to her was that praise from the lonely old woman for the man they both loved. I myself found praise for him too. The reward I sought, however, was the thanks in Annie's eyes.

While I was speaking the old woman's farm manager came in accompanied by a young man.

"Here is a young man," said the manager, "who took part in the Rising too. He was lifted and was sent overseas. It's only a few days since he was released. He has come here on a visit with news for you."

This, I thought, is the end of the lying. The stranger would have the truth of the story and he would tell it in his own stupid clumsy way. For the mother who had been longing for the return of her son this would be the end.

I looked at Annie. I could not understand why she showed no signs of anxiety.

The stranger began to tell his tale.

"Four days ago I left Frongoch," he began. "I was told to come here on a visit. I had become very friendly with your son, Richard."

This certainly startled me. What mental confusion, I asked myself, had come over me? Was the man who died by my side on a house-top in Dublin one and the same person as the son of the woman sitting there like a stone statue?

The stranger continued with his story.

"He was the heart of all our fun; the beginning and end of our merriment; a ray of sunshine in a dark cave."

The talk and the praise ran on. Motionless, the mother listened. Shortly afterwards the three of us bade goodbye to the old woman, but the stranger promised he would come again.

"Again and again, my dear lady," he assured her. "Never would I tire of speaking of that brave man, of Richard of the big heart — that's what we called him in the camp. Never till my dying day could I weary of telling you about him."

On our way from the great house I asked the stranger, "Where were you in the fight?"

"Never have I fought except on the stage of a theatre. Nor, if I can manage it, shall I ever fight anywhere else."

"But haven't you said you've just come out of Frongoch?"

"Frongoch!" he exclaimed, throwing his arms wide as though he were on a stage. "Frongoch! I care not for you. The harsh mountain air around that place would not suit my lungs. The stagnant air of a swamp! — I'd hate it."

"And how long did you spend there?" I asked.

"Never was my body there but my soul has hovered over that camp since our brave warriors were first incarcerated there," and he struck an attitude as though he were about to declaim twenty times as much when Annie interrupted.

"It was I who brought him here," she said quietly. "I was afraid the old woman was becoming suspicious. If any doubt were to enter her heart nothing would drive it out. Her old heart would be torn asunder."

I looked at her. In this wonderful world is there anything stranger than a woman?

*

Have you ever spent much time in the company of the

blind? The person who is blind from birth or even from early youth, does not turn his face from you while speaking. But the person who became blind when on in years usually tries to look at you when he is moved by anxiety or deep emotion. Such a person lacks knowledge of and is unfamiliar with the kingdom of the blind. He does not see the brightness of enchantment nor the wonders. He has one foot in our world and the other foot beyond. And the pity of Mary is the person who is between the two worlds.

But this was not so with the old woman. Hers was the true insight of the blind. No matter what you might say to her, no matter what she herself might say, you would imagine from her that she knew exactly the uneven byways of the country of the blind; and she "saw" the magic light that is hidden from the rest of us; that around her was a barrier impossible to scale.

And as she lost strength and vigour while the autumn stole from us and the days of frost and cold drew closer, so the wall rose higher between her and the busy world. Annie felt the old woman held a secret and she was tense and afraid lest it should be the secret of our lying. I, however, did not think that this was so.

"She is a woman apart." I said. "No one has found it possible to come close to the life and soul within her. She has not changed except that she is becoming more and more accustomed and responsive to the mysterious world of the blind."

But that apart, her health was getting worse. By November she was unable to leave the house and the greater part of each day was spent in bed. Often in the morning I would go in to talk to her. There I would meet Annie and we used to spend the early part of the night as well chatting to her until she would fall into a light broken slumber.

And then both of us would steal away, trying to guess
what was in the old woman's heart. I at least had my
own opinion. Had she not on one occasion pressed Annie's
hand in mine? And for a short while had she not held our
two hands together in her own?

"What meaning had she in doing that," Annie asked
me on our way home that night, "if she believes that
Richard is alive?"

"What meaning could she have," I asked, "other than
that there should be a friendly understanding between
the three of us until Richard would return."

Annie looked at me. It seemed to me that she did not
accept my explanation. She blushed too — sorry, perhaps,
that she had spoken.

*

And so the time passed. One morning I read in the paper
that the prisoners who were in Frongoch were to be
released. My heart rose. Soon I would see some of my old
friends again. I hurried to tell the good news to Annie.
When she read the item she immediately became anxious.

"She will know now," she said. "She will know now
that she is without a son and that since the summer we
have been lying to her. This will kill her."

"Let us hurry then," said I, "and warn the people of
the house not to tell her."

We did so and then called on the old woman. From her
demeanour we were unable to say whether or not she had
heard the news. She was clearly very feeble now — weak
from the world — yet, nonetheless, a strange unearthly
energy seemed to possess her.

"I was hoping you would come," she said, "for I have
good news for you."

We were both startled. She knew then that the prisoners

were coming home. She would be expecting her beloved son in a few days. When he would not arrive she would know the deceit that had been practised on her. This would be the end.

"I have good news for you," the old woman repeated. "In a few days I shall see my dear son again."

Annie and I looked at each other. What had we better do?

"Annie," said the old woman, "go out and tell the manager to have everything in readiness for him when my son comes."

Annie left the room. The piteous look she gave me as she went out!

The old woman clutched me by the shoulder.

"Whisper! Whisper!" she said, and one would hardly recognise her voice. I put my ear close to her lips.

"I shall see my son soon — perhaps in a couple of days."

She checked herself, her breath coming shortly.

"I'll see him," she said, "but not in this world. I am dying. He is near. My son is near."

Because of the emotion that shook her she could say no more for a time. After a while she spoke again.

"I knew all along that he had been killed — I knew it — but I would not tell it to Annie — it would kill her — break her heart — the love those two had for each other!"

Those women! Each one of them trying to deceive the other lest the news of the death of the man they both loved should break the heart of either.

I did not tell her that Annie knew also.

"When I am gone," the old woman said, "you may tell her the story — you may tell her that my son died — that my son died for Ireland . . . ."

And I have never seen a prouder look on anyone's face.

Two days afterwards that proud heroic old woman died. Annie and I attended the funeral.

"A courageous woman," Annie remarked to me on our way home.

"Like yourself," I said to her.

"Like her son," said Annie.

I know that all three of them had courage. I myself have courage too; a kind of courage. But I have not yet got the courage to tell Annie of the love I have for her.

What would you advise me to do?

My Poet, Dark and Slender

translated by Bryan MacMahon

I

A few slim volumes of verse containing poems that fire
the imagination with their sheer beauty, that's all we
have left nowadays to remind us of the life and work of
dark-haired Burke — a man who followed the trade of
poetry in Dublin in our own times. Yes, indeed, a few
slender offerings, difficult enough to come by these recent
days — that's all that remains of the poet except perhaps
a bitter memory in a woman's heart.

Once upon a time his friends had high hopes for his
future. Wherever you go these latter days, if people are
discussing the Easter Rising you're bound to hear someone ask — "Whatever happened to Burke, the poet with
the dark hair? And tell me, what part exactly did he play
in the historic events of Easter '16?"

And when the enquirer is told that the man did abso-
lutely nothing except scribble a few lines in praise of the
men who fought, everyone reacts in amazement. Not that
Burke is ever criticised, and that's an outstanding tribute
to the sympathetic nature and tolerance of the Irish
people, for if anyone deserved to be castigated Burke did,
for he betrayed his own gospel by failing to bear witness
to it, especially since he got the clear opportunity to do
so.

Of course, you'll meet many people who'll tell you precisely the type of man he was when he first made his appearance in Dublin City. They tell you how profoundly he moved women with his high-flown talk and the flash of his grey-green eye. And how he urged men into action with the fire and balance of his mind. These are the two most commonplace verdicts on the man. There's many a woman too whose cheeks glow and whose eyes glisten at the mention of his name and if you gain the confidence of one of these she'll tell you of the high esteem in which she once held him. But if you have the slightest insight into what goes on deep in a woman's heart, you'll know at once that this womanly esteem is very much akin to love.

Then again there are other women who'll offer you all kinds of excuses as to why the poet failed to strike a blow at the time when it was sorely needed, and if you can convince them that it wasn't for lack of courage he failed to act, then these women will be your friends until you go into the grave.

I met seven women recently: each of the seven knew the poet. Some were close friends of his: others knew him only by sight. But each of the seven spent quite a long time discussing him with me.

Three mentioned the rare quality of his poetry — these three knew him indirectly only. Two others, in their reticent and womanly way, praised the fine appearance of the man — I told myself that praise like this was a sure sign of affection. There was another woman and every titbit of scandal about him, she had it right on the tip of her tongue. And yet another woman, the seventh I met, harboured venom in the depths of her heart for the poet. It was almost the cause of breaking a lifetime of friendship between us when I ventured to put in a good word for him; when I did so she cut me short by telling me the following tale.

The Woman's Tale

Where's the use in talking? What good does it do you to try to excuse him! If anyone knew him I did! Burke the Bard with magic in his eyes and the sweet nimble word on his lips, ever ready to play up to women! I knew him well: I knew him in a way few women knew him. God forbid that any woman should know any man like him — his body and soul — ever, ever again.

I had been five years married when I first saw him. I was childless. My husband — what can I do but admit that the pair of us were sick of each other. Sick and tired — that's a proper description of our relationship. Now, I didn't hate the man: if I *did* hate him we could possibly have whiled away the long nights bickering and wrangling. But how could a woman quarrel with a man in whom she wasn't even interested? Apathy and disinterest — these were the twin cankers in our lives.

When a woman is thirty, without children, tied to a placid, easygoing man and has plenty of the world's goods, one would think that she could live a fine soft life in a city like this. But just look around you! There are literally hundreds of well-off wives passing agreeable but trivial existences, what with shopping expeditions in the afternoon and tea which is an excuse for tongue-lashing their neighbours and their friends. Then there's the train home to dinner to find their lord and master snoring over a newspaper. My stomach turns when I think of it.

That's exactly the kind of life I led until I met Dark-haired Burke, maker of verses and ditcher of women!

You can't have lived in Dublin during that period

without hearing of the dances that were held in the Rhymers' Rooms. You'd meet all Dublin there, rather, anyone with any kind of a reputation. Poets? Don't mention poets to me! The place was bulging with them. You'd have to keep a sharp look-out or one of them would pounce on you and never let you go until he had recited a long dreary poem into your ear.

As far as I remember, it was Betty who took me there in the first place. I have to giggle now when I think of the dress Betty wore that night. A Fancy Dress affair — every one who attended had to pretend he or she was someone else. Poor Betty went as a schoolgirl. Barefooted, if you please! Wouldn't you imagine that a woman whose feet are chapped with chilblains and skinny into the bargain would never dream of going barefooted in male company. But Betty didn't care — you see, she already had a man!

There we were, the pair of us, sitting down at the upper end of the dance hall, chewing away on a nice juicy scrap of scandal when we saw him coming towards us. He was dressed as a soldier of Garibaldi, red blouse and all — and I needn't tell you that such a uniform suits a tall good-looking swarthy man. In mid-floor his foot kind of slipped but neither that nor the amused reaction of those who noticed it took the slightest bit from his dignity. He just tightened his lips, his face paled and he looked around him pretty boldly at those who had reacted with smiles to his mis-step. I liked him at once! I caught Betty's hand and had begun to ask who he was; before she had time to answer he was standing right beside me.

His head was as well-shapen as ever sat on a man; yes, head, neck and shoulders too. If I hadn't caught Betty's hand I would have noticed his feet and his knees. For he was as flat-footed as any tramp walking the roads. You know me well, and you know my weakness — that I can't, as they say, 'warm' to one who is heavy and awkward on his feet, but in some indefinable way this man could succeed in distracting one's attention from his single blemish.

He spoke to Betty — every one knew Betty — but even as he did so his eyes were fast on me. His unusual eyes held me as in a vice. They bored right through me and I could read stark passion in those same two eyes.

There and then I was taken with a kind of awe. I wanted to creep away and hide myself in some corner at the world's end. I couldn't move! I was a hooked fish. No chance of escape! Before I knew where I was, the pair of us were in mid-floor dancing, dancing, dancing.

That dance! Terror overcomes me when I think of it. I shiver in every limb and my heart begins to pound. I don't imagine that this type of dance had ever before been seen in Dublin — in red hot African countries, yes, where among dark-skinned natives it was first practised, so as to offer thanks to a god of fertility. Why did I do it? you well may ask. I can't answer that question. I suppose it roused some old demon in my inmost core. Here was a man who was hunting me in the old primitive way. So as to tame me! And that's exactly what gave me pleasure! I wanted to set him on fire, to rouse out the passion of his body, then to subdue him and stamp him underfoot.

All this was a delusion, of course! The music, created to incite passion, the close atmosphere of the hall, the touch of skin on skin, the twists and turns of the barbaric dance and his eyes — those eyes of his set so close to mine, edged as they were with unearthly fire, how could a weak woman like myself defend herself, a woman, too, whose younger days were spent in the presence of music and beauty with every comfort and pleasure of life beneath fragrant blue Eastern Skies.

On occasions like this, eyes communicate far better than speech. And are more powerful than speech! My eyes surrendered to his and when that happens that's the beginning and end of the story. Dark Burke knew this well: the music stopped abruptly, the dance was over, and there the pair of us stood in mid-floor with an uncanny understanding of the dark riddle that shall never be solved. I found myself growing afraid. So did he, I think.

Now you've often visited the Pleasure Garden — it's right opposite the Rhymers' Rooms. No more intimate place in the whole of Dublin. It was May — May of the blossoms and mingled scents. There hung in the night air a heavy fragrance that dulled the senses: it emanated from clay and fresh growth. Starlets both mocking and solemn looked down on us; the distant din of the city drummed in our ears like the boom of a spring tide. A faint puff of wind, charged with night scents sieved down from the mountains and began to make free with my shoulders and throat — then as if jealous of the caprice of the breeze the man caught my cloak and drew it close about my shoulders, his fingers got caught in my hair, his right hand dallied on my neck and all the while he was looking intensely into my eyes. An issue of warmth, a glare of lightning passed through my limbs.

Tell me this! Whatever you do, don't tell me a lie! Does this sudden wrench at the heart affect the man as it does the woman? Does fire pulse through his veins in the same way as this current moved through my veins on this occasion?

At the end of the Garden there's a small lake, a fine ash tree growing beside it and a seat in its shade. We sat down there. Both of us hadn't said a word since we left the hall. He was looking out over the water and the starlight that glittered on its surface. He was gazing also at the utter darkness, at the far bank where hawthorns and shrubs grew at the verge of the water. I was watchful:

one-third fearful, two-thirds afraid. Whom or what I was expecting I won't reveal.

He raised his head. He glanced up at the sky. The light was adequate: I could see his forehead in profile. I'd wager that never a woman — if she was womanly — looked at that forehead of his without paying its owner the keenest attention. I thought every minute that he was going to speak, that he was about to explain the witchery and eeriness of the night and of that particular occasion in words shining and poetic. If at that moment he had poured out these words in a torrent; if he had taken me in his arms and grasped me as a nettle is grasped, I was completely his. There I was, all agog for poetry and praise, even for seduction and gentle cajolery.

Not for long! Whatever turn he gave, the pocket of his jacket struck against the seat. Out popped a bottle and fell to the ground. It broke into smithereens.

"Hell!" shouted the poet with one eye on myself.

The man was right to explode. And what else am I but a complete idiot to be talking to you like this.

Pouff! All the sex and strangeness that lay between us ever since we had met were put to flight by that honest exclamation.

Gone also was the mood which had taken us ever since we had danced together. Now, we understood each other.

Oh, but we got to know each other better! I knew from his carriage and the way he spoke that he was poetic in the truest sense of the word but I had never even read a single line he had written. To be candid I barely knew what he wrote — scraps of verses in the newspapers and things like that. But his voice — useless for me to try to describe it. He recited a short poem for me, something about a saint — I never fancied saints, I couldn't understand the way they lived — but the saint whom the poet described, I understood his heart as well as I did my own.

II

Before long people began to take notice of the marked change that was gradually coming over me, they saw that my health was improving and that I was growing more cheerful than I was before: I was even told that I was getting younger every day. It was true. I had a first-class physician — poetry and peril, the finest physic for a woman in my situation. So I had the wide world of healing right at my fingertips.

The poet and myself seemed to be meeting everywhere. Before this no place on earth would do him but a bar-room. Now if he happened to hear that I was to visit such and such a house, say for a cup of tea or a chat, he'd arrive before the end of my visit and convey me home.

People talked of course: in fact they talked their heads off, but we didn't care for we were fully engrossed in our own enjoyable and self-sufficient world. So when the lovely amber summer came round we two filled it with poetry and charm, with love and ringing laughter.

What a time we had that summer! And how we came to know each other! It dawns on me now that during that season every particle of happiness in his personality greatly increased. You've probably read the book of poetry he published that year — well, every poem it contains was written for me and for me alone!

Is it any wonder then that I began, as it were, to shed my years? Back came my full health and my former merry outlook on life. Everyone remarked on it, that is, everyone except my husband! How on earth could he notice it, since the man was completely absorbed in his business affairs and in his collection of butterflies.

Yes indeed, thousands and thousands of butterflies of

every type, hue and classification. What did a man like that want a wife for? About this time too he had got his hands on a few specimens that gladdened his heart and you've never seen anyone so proud! The old boyos who travelled with him every morning on the nine o'clock train thought that he was delighted because of my being restored to health. Some of them went so far as to congratulate him on my recovery — the simpletons.

Betty happened to be right there in the carriage one morning. She told me about all the talk — and the gossip. There's a better version of the incident than the one Betty gave. That soft lob, Toohey from Dun Laoire, you know him don't you? — he's the fellow who's always knocking about with Sheila Redmond — well he began asking Aymonn (that's the pet name I have for my husband — I call him this because of his likeness to a family coachman of that name we had several years ago) a whole lot of questions. That fat lump of blubber quizzing my husband as to who was the doctor I attended and who did me so much good, and letting on that he got no relief from his own doctor, he thought maybe that this doctor of mine would bring him relief. Everyone in the carriage of course knew how matters stood and there they were smirking and winking behind their newspapers.

The doctor who cured me? Didn't the wide world know that I attended no doctor except my poet, dark and slender. They even thought my husband didn't know, and to be candid I thought so myself at that time. A man apart, a very unusual man with a deep and intricate personality, very few people understood you, Aymonn.

Whatever about that, when he came home that evening and the two of us were sitting at the fireside after the evening meal he was in a very thoughtful mood indeed. From time to time he glanced sharply in my direction — to me his eyes were like piercing awls. But then again perhaps my conscience was troubling me and I was imagining things that didn't exist.

After a while, "By the way," he began, "someone asked me the name of your doctor today." His voice was soft and unruffled.

I was taken aback. "Oh . . . ." I faltered. The word "doctor" had knocked me off balance, simply because I had often mentioned to my dark poet that no doctor on earth had done me as much good as he. I suddenly got the impression that Aymonn had heard all sorts of things about me, and further, that the worst possible construction had been put on matters, so I braced myself for the clash of temperaments, the war of words and the rumpus. Perhaps matters wouldn't stop there!

"That doctor?" His gaze going through me and not a flicker of emotion on his expression.

I find my head reeling; My thoughts are utterly confused. And still I cling to the conviction that I will not be unmasked. The fact that I had taken a few small parts in Abbey Theatre productions now stood me in good stead.

"That doctor? By rights . . . ." he persisted.

The climax was near. And when it came the consequences would be dire! I knew that he kept a handgun of sorts: as I watched, I realized that one of his hands was thrust into his pocket. I kept one eye firmly fixed on that hand. I asked myself if the bullet would go right through my forehead. I hoped it would not, for in that event my face would be disfigured. And a vain woman like myself didn't take kindly to the prospect of a blemish, even in the tomb! Would I fare better if I blurted out the whole story? What would the consequences be? Would Aymonn make allowances for me? Would he believe what I had to say? Would he even remotely understand? Again, could I avoid the danger by making a clean breast of everything?

The hand went deeper into the pocket. Here it comes, I told myself.

Take that smile off your face. Put your hand on my heart. There it goes pounding like anything. Even now I look back with terror on that moment.

As Aymonn stood up, I whispered the Act of Sorrow. But again I had made up my mind, even if it cost me my life, not to betray my poet. Would I hear the explosion before I died? I began to count one, two, three, four. . . .

Not a word, I say! How could I expect anything else You must have read enough of the romantic fiction of today to know that a husband could do nothing else with a wife like me — that is if the authors are to be believed. And then — listen! You simply must believe me. He said: "I hope the maid doesn't burn the porridge to-night!"

I scuttled straight out of the room and threw myself down on a chair in the kitchen. I laughed and cried in one single howl of relief. Then I cried and laughed, turn and turn about so that I didn't know whether I was laughing or crying.

Was there ever, ever such a man!

He called out to me. Back I came! "Sit down," he said. I sat down.

"Where do you spend most of your time these days?" he asked.

Off goes my poor heart again. I wasn't out of the wood by any means. But now I had more confidence than before. Perhaps it was because I had put the worst of the ordeal over me in the kitchen. Again I toyed with the notion of telling everything. And wasn't I the happy woman that the truth wasn't worse than it was. No, no . . . . that isn't my philosophy of life at all. You see, I hold that this world exists so that I can knock a whack of enjoyment out of it. So now, if I was forced to tell Aymonn the truth, it was only the shame that mattered. This is, *if* I was forced to tell!

Am I making myself clear? But then again, I simply hadn't to confess a single thing — this I quickly realized as soon as he opened his mouth.

"I find you somehow .... getting younger, Eileen. For the past three or four months you look the picture of health. Day by day the colour creeps back into your cheeks. It's as if you were filled with the music and gaiety of life. The old gloom is gone. Depression and weariness have lifted."

His tone of voice was so intimate and affectionate, as indeed was the way in which his eyes rested on me, that I found myself on the point of explaining the reason for my recovery. Before I could speak, he gestured to me to stop.

"No need to explain the reason for the change. I know it. I knew it from the start. I know the doctor who healed you — yes, indeed, even though the fools in the railway carriage thought I didn't. The only thing I regret is that I wasn't the man to bring about the change in you."

As if overcome with sadness, he was silent for a while.

"Let's not bother with it any more tonight," he went on. "You now know exactly how matters stand between us. How they have stood between us since the very beginning."

I found myself sighing.

"That's all I have to say! Let's leave it at that. Simply that! I'm well aware what made you well again and who caused your recovery. I've no intention of mentioning his name until you first mention it yourself. I'm not blind to his qualities — his seven talents I should have said: his poetic gift, his sense of patriotism, his fine appearance, his loyalty. . . ."

Praise like this for my beloved poet was the sweetest

music I have heard since my wedding day. I almost kissed
the man! I stopped short as he went on:

"I also heard of his notoriety. His fondness for drink
and women."

I made as if to say something but he wouldn't have it.
To this day, I lose my temper when anyone mentions my
lover's reputation as regards women. Can you tell me
why on earth this is so?

"But even though he has those seven. . . . claims to
fame, I still say that I'm thankful to him. He brought you
peace of mind. And even if he does have the reputation
of being a womanizer, I still trust you. And will always
do so."

There were his two eyes boring right through me. Was
it a blessing from God that, so far, I hadn't a whole lot to
hide? He called my name, then broke off. Again, those
plaintive eyes of his touching me to my inmost being.
Had there been even the slightest spark of love between
us, it would have blazed up at that moment.

Aren't the ways of God most complicated?

"Bring him here . . . . to this house!" Aymonn went on.
"For your sake I'll make him welcome." At the doorway
he paused for a while looking back at me. "I'm truly
sorry that I cannot take his place in your affections. That
I would dearly like to do . . . ." He turned as if to go but
quickly returned.

"A final word of advice." He was framed in the doorway. His tone of voice had changed. "If you are to meet
him tonight, just be careful. The night air has its hazards
so guard against a . . . . lapse. Again I tell you . . . . bring
him here!"

He left the room in his own quick way without saying
another word.

I dressed myself. Yes, I had an appointment with my
dark man of the songs. Passing the window of the room

in which my husband was, I happened to glance in. There
he was, standing at the table, a magnifying glass glued to
his eye, minutely examining one of his beloved butterflies.

Men!

III

Look! You were in love with a woman once. I don't have
to tell you how a lover hurries when there is good news
for the loved one. I honestly don't know what means of
transport I had — maybe it was a magic carpet from the
East! Or I could have been borne aloft on the wings of
my wonderful tale.

He was there before me — at the corner of the top of
Grafton Street. Right there, standing under a street lamp
with an open book in his hands. The passers-by had to
walk right around him — he was like a solid rock in the
middle of a stream of human beings.

"Hallo," I said. He returned the salute: it's hard to
describe the sense of dignity he could convey at times. He
could raise his hat in a special way as if the manners of
the French and the loyalty of the Irish were combined in
one person.

"So your new book is out," I said. "Isn't it quite a
large volume?"

"It's not that at all," he said, handing me the book.

The sight almost left my eyes! You wouldn't guess what
the book was about if you were at it forever. It was a large
scientific tome dealing with above all things, the life-cycle
of butterflies!

Dead silence as we walked along. Crossing O'Connell
Bridge I recovered my speech.

"Are you interested in butterflies . . . . too?" I squeaked.
It gave me all I could do to ask the question. There

was my man at home interested in nothing in the world except those infernal insects. And now, here was my poet, dark and slender playing the same damn tune.

I asked God to blast all butterflies off the face of the earth.

"That book? Oh — yes. . . ." He didn't get the chance to explain his interest in this particular branch of the sciences, for at that moment a man passing by saluted him and had a few quiet words with him. That same man will never again be seen — this side of the grave.

I walked on with my poet. "I'll explain about the book when we get into the Theatre," he said.

Have you ever walked O'Connell Street in one of those golden days in the company of a famous poet or politician? Together, we two were like a royal couple parading their capital city immediately after the ceremony of coronation. That was exactly how we walked, myself and my bard, the dark and slender one.

Until that night, I never properly understood the respect and awe in which people held him. Every five yards or so some one would salute him — women mostly, I couldn't help noticing. And every woman he greeted (and it was very few he didn't!) had a single unspoken question on her lips: who is the strange woman always seen nowadays in the company of Burke the Poet? What influence has she over him — eh? Devil another woman is he interested in now except her ladyship!

Or: Is that her? Will you give one look at the dowdy dress she's wearing. Ah, I have you now . . . . a queer tale and no mistake about it.

Or: It isn't possible. That one! And to think of all the poetry he has written — about the beauty of women.

As if I cared what they said! Hadn't I my slender dark poet for my very own! And if the women were jealous they had good reason for being so. Before very long,

however, my pride took a tumble. I heard a passer-by
— a woman — pass a remark.

"You'd never notice his deformity in the dark," - that's
what she said. And if I were alone, as likely as not, I'd
have caught her and dragged her by the hair.

My rhymer started tongue-lashing the woman but he
did so in such a spate of words that I couldn't quite follow
him. He must have overheard the remark and it cut him
to the quick. I had pity for him: but of course you must
allow for the fact that I was head over heels in love with
him those days and this flaw of his didn't trouble me in
the least.

And to think of the revulsion I formerly experienced
for a blemish of this sort!

IV

As for the book on Entomology which my slender poet
had with him that night a word of explanation is needed.

Here in this box I have a diary which I kept during
that period. No one has ever seen it: I'll read a few lines
for you now. Don't you know why I do this?

Listen! And no nonsense if you please.

Hallowe'en. (I wrote very little in my diary that year,
but let that pass.) In the Abbey Theatre with my loved
one. A drama by J. M. Synge. My very first time seeing
the play. Didn't pay much attention to it at first. Never
heard of the playwright before. A little upset because of
my conversation with Aymonn and of course this new
"science" my darling is interested in — those abominable
butterflies!

Before long I feel a hand in mine. Fingers pressing on
my fingers. I hear a low musical voice — that of my poet,
dark and slender.

"I want you to listen, Eileen."

I listened. I was expecting, I suppose, soft soothery words — lyrical words too — to match the occasion with the clasp of a hand in mine. But if I expected a poetic response I got exactly what I sought, not from the man beside me but from an actor on the stage.

Up there a travelling man was talking to a woman whose husband was being waked. He was trying to persuade her to run off with him.

"Come along with me, lady of the house," he was saying, "and together we'll walk at nightfall in the dark woods of mystery where the stars of heaven will glimmer down upon us, where we lie side by side in the shadow of the bushes. And daybreak will come upon us and birdsong will enliven the green branches". I pressed the poet's fingers. Then I snatched away my hand at once fearing that he would interpret the gesture as an indication that I was eager to hear a similar invitation from his lips.

I was now taken by the oddest of moods. My companion sensed my feeling of emotion: it was as if an electric current or feeling of absolute sympathy had passed between us. I knew that his eyes were fast upon me in the half-light of the theatre, that they were drugging my senses and that such a glance spelled danger for us both. I realized that if I chanced to look deep into his eyes I would see the craving of his heart and spirit. I was aware that, body and soul, he hungered for me, that, as it were, rays of fire emanated from him. caressing me, but scorching and torturing me as well. I was moved utterly by the power implicit in those eyes.

But then, at the critical moment, the curtain came down on the stage, the lights went up and the final music began. My first attempt to speak to him was a failure. I began to consider whether or not I would mention the conversation I **had** had with **my** husband. Again I fal-

tered. He seemed to understand the reason for my failure
and also conveyed the impression that he knew I was
aware of his understanding. But he made no move to help
me out. I came to the conclusion that he wanted to
maintain whatever emotional advantage he held over me.

Only for the butterfly book we'd have had no topic of
conversation to fall back on — this although my heart
and my spirit were overflowing with emotion.

"You've an interest in butterflies, I see?" The book
was in my hand.

"Yes — and no!"

I would have questioned him with my eyes but I knew
that my little "turn" was not yet over.

"You're the cause of my having the book," he said.

"I'm the cause?"

He went on to explain. He said that he was due to visit
such and such a house. He knew that my husband would
be there also. So he wanted to have some knowledge of
butterflies so that he'd be in a position to discuss the
subject with some authority — something very few Dub-
liners could do. And then — I'm thoroughly ashamed to
admit this weakness in my poet, dark and slender — he
felt sure that the conversation would result in his receiving
an invitation to my home.

Be sure of one thing, I now told myself! I have no
intention whatsoever of telling my poet that he already
has had an invitation to visit us. That spells danger and
dire danger! And there's also the fact that my husband
trusts me. But wait, what happens if I'm asked at home
why my poet hasn't accepted the invitation? Difficulties
whatever way I turn.

Those two men!

V

Here is a further extract from the diary.

Betty dropped in to see me in the afternoon. She "clipped" the neighbours' reputation — I enjoyed it greatly. But then she went on for a solid hour to pour vials of wrath on the head of my poet friend.

Wild horses wouldn't stop Betty once she gets really started on the reputations of others. Every word out of her mouth then conveys a double meaning and if one pulls her up to question her, she declares that that is not what she meant to convey at all, but the very opposite if you please! Her comments leave an ugly taste in the mouth: you're left with a sense of mistrust in the person discussed no matter how well you thought of him previous to this.

She tells horrible little tales about anyone she dislikes. Then, all of a sudden she stops and says:

"I've no right to tell you this! Considering how great you are with him!"

She leaves you brooding. The one you admire comes badly out of it. It could be that the woman is jealous simply because the poet and I are in love. And then again, it could hardly be that she detests the man. I daresay the truth of the matter is that she's pinched and perished by nature and can't stand anyone being happier than she is. Dog-in-the-Manger, I forget who it was wrote that fable, but I have the book somewhere in the house and post it to her I shall this very evening! And the next time she calls to see me I'll make sure *not* to be available even if it causes me to miss the gossip of the city.

I'm sorry to the heart that I ever took her into my confidence. But I had to have a friend — a woman confessor to whom I could confide my inmost secrets. But again, wasn't I the unfortunate woman to trust her; why, oh why, are such female types never done trying to tie a knot closer than the knot of friendship? And to think of all this kissing and hugging that goes on whenever I spin them a lonesome story! But I have the solution! My husband will be the truest of my friends — he really is an extraordinary man — and also I'll have my poet as my lover, forever and ever.

Forever! How Betty would howl with laughter if she could read those lines. Forever! And to think of all the sweethearts I've had already!

Twenty? Maybe! Honestly, I'm too exhausted to-night to start counting them, but the Lord knows that not one of them could compare with my poet, dark and slender. But on second thoughts I ask myself, what standards of comparison do I have? Hm . . . . Ever since Betty opened her big mouth my brain keeps going round and round. Is he as wicked as people say? Does he care for me at all? Does he simply want my body . . . . and no more?

And that Butterfly book! I go crazy when I think that he took the trouble of buying it and that now he's bursting with knowledge for the sole purpose of hoodwinking my husband. That's why he fished for the invitation . . . . so as, finally, to deceive me in the old, old way.

Here's his photograph right in front of me as I write these lines. I keep asking myself how it is that sensuality and lust, folly and intelligence, meanness and highmindedness can co-exist behind the screen of his fine brow. But, no matter, I prefer him to any man born. I will kiss my Satan with kisses, one two three.

O Lord in Heaven!

I'll leave the house now. Yes, he will meet and speak to me in his old brilliant way. The dark clouds will scatter. Doubts will vanish. I'll have him all to myself.

So, poet, dark and slender, dear dear one, master of charm and beauty, I am yours and yours alone in flesh and in spirit. And whether you're damned or glorified doesn't make the slightest difference to me.

N.B. Men are forbidden ever to read these lines.

VI

I never saw such a man in my life!

Well, here I am sitting without a word out of me for fully ten minutes waiting for you to ask me a certain question. And not a word out of you!

What question, you ask! I'll tell you. You never asked what dress I was wearing on any of the occasions I walked out with my poetic friend. I wouldn't mind, but you, above all people know the full range of my wardrobe.

I'm sorely tempted to stop talking at this point and to tell you no more. But I'd scorn to play a trick like that on you, for you're a nice person, a very nice person — in your own kind of way, that is.

Yes, I met my minstrel on the very same night as Betty paid me that visit. Just as I had anticipated, I was hooked on the spot. I found myself both animated and excited; I had lost control of myself. He knew this at once: I never in my life met anyone with the intuition he had in that kind of situation — I found it uncanny. When I was that way I was clay in his hands. And well he knew it.

A tram was coming. He caught my arm. Before I quite realized it I was sitting side by side with him on the top of that tram. The conductor came along.

"Two to Rathfarnham," my companion said.

"Wait!" I said. "I'm not going that far."

He took the tickets. The conductor passed on. We were alone. I made as if to get up and go, but thought better of it. I was somewhat afraid of him. Or of myself.

"Sit where you are!" he said. Authoritatively. I sat where I was. Why ask me why I obeyed. Even now I haven't the faintest idea why I did so. He was certainly the master of the situation. And don't believe any woman who says she can't stand a masterful man. I made a second attempt to get to my feet.

"Look, Eileen," he began and I knew by his tone of voice that he was still in command. "Tonight, let's see what the woods are like."

Half-heartedly from me, "I meant to spend only a quarter of an hour with you."

"The dark oak woods," he went on as if he hadn't heard a word I said.

Then he started to hold forth. Such beautiful poetic speech: he surpassed himself this time. Was it any wonder that I was mesmerized?

I often noticed that at times like this his forehead betrayed him. It indicated that at one moment he could look like an animal and then, quick as a wink, the cultured poet was back again. He had already indicated this change between the time I met him and the time we reached the woods.

There's an oak grove in Rathfarnham: it's about a quarter of a mile off the road with a cluster of pine trees around it. All you can see in there is a patch of the night sky far above.

There we sat. Creatures from the nether-world moved around us — if only we had eyes to see them. Stirred by the wind the trees raised a lament for the dead.

I was somewhat annoyed at this moment. I had come there more or less against my will. On the other hand I was glad to be near him, now that he wore his mask of happiness. He appeared calm and thoughtful with not a trace of evil in his face.

Suddenly, "My life is in tatters!" he broke in. "And you are to blame."

I couldn't hold back the laughter. Why? you ask.

Because I was thinking of the many men who had already said something like that to me. And not one of them meant a word of it!

There was a flicker of anger in his eye. Outwardly he remained calm. Not so with me!

"Perhaps tonight you'd rather have poetry than philosophy," he said. Then off he trots reciting a short poem in a beautiful sincere tone of voice. Well, blast the man anyway, the poem he recited was one he had made for the woman he was great with at that particular time. Betty is my author for this. And the same day that Betty told me that she also told me how the lady fared — when the poet tired of her.

"Did she do away with herself?" I asked with mock innocence. Somehow or other, I was bent on rousing the man.

"Who?"

I retailed the whole story just as I had heard it. "And I don't want poetry or any damn thing tonight," I shouted, and added "I'm off!" He caught me as I got up.

"You're not going!" he said. There before me was his mad-dog face.

We struggled. The ground came up to meet me. I lost all power to resist. Now I hate him with an insensate hate.

Let me read another passage for you:

Haven't laid eyes on him since that night in the grove. Now I am completely confused. I'm sick, sick, sick. I haven't left the bed for a week and no one knows what's the matter with me.

Times I tell myself that I'll never speak to him again: times I long for him. He's Satan in human form. But again, whether devil or human being he certainly holds all my feeling in an unbreakable grip. I'll write him and tell him to come right here. I'll do it now, this instant.

What good would that do me? How many letters have I written to him withing the past month, telling him alternately that I hated him, that I loved him. Letters that were never posted. I daresay I'll never lay eyes on him again.

What's that? That noise! That explosion! What's that you say? A rebellion? A rebellion, is that what you say? In the name of heavens, have sense! Gunfire? The Volunteers? Good Lord, that couldn't possibly be true.

Talk, talk, that's all it is, talk. How often have I told my poet that the day was gone when anyone would raise a hand for Ireland's sake. Nothing but talk, everlasting talk.

There go the guns again to give me the lie. I think of my dark slender poet, in the brunt of the battle.

My husband has just come in. "It's true," he tells me. "You'd never imagine that that crowd would have had the courage to rise!"

"My friend, the poet. . . ." the words slipped out of my mouth.

"Another good physician gone," my husband remarks drily as he goes out the door.

"There goes a man devoid of feeling," I tell myself.

No sleep that night. I am proud of my people. Proud that they rose against the old enemy. May the courage of my people be praised forever!

Give me manhood! Give me back my health! Give me the strength even to stand erect and I'd be side by side with my poet where the fight is fiercest. I seem to see him in mid-battle, his comrades around him. He is the leader . . . .he is the inspiration.

Dear God! Now I imagine I see him lying dead. His noble face upturned to the sky, a smile of victory on his lips. . . .a bullet through his heart. His name is immortal. All his faults are forgiven. Even I forgive you your sins, brave one, lover, secret. Imagination saps my strength. Suddenly I wake. My husband is leaning over me. He speaks my name. Far more affectionately than ever before.

(I had spent the day in delirium talking wildly about my lover. I was trying vainly to rise to my feet so as to embrace his beautiful body. It was late in the evening when I recovered somewhat.)

Aymonn was seated on the edge of the bed. He was there for quite a while, if only I had known. His hand was on my forehead. "Don't worry," he said "your friend will be back."

"Never!"

Again, his gentle voice. "I'm going into the city. I know a man who appears to know exactly what's going on. I won't come back until I have word for you."

A kiss! Then almost before I realized it he was gone. Suddenly I see that my husband is risking his life trying to bring me news of my lover. Did ever such a generous man walk the earth?

VIII

I don't have to read any more. You know as well as myself how matters ended. No need to tell you that I'm now a widow. They found Aymonn's body in a laneway near Portobello. The bullet had passed right through his head.

And what about my poet, dark and slender?

Is there one in Dublin who hasn't seen him lately? No one, for he's everywhere. Telling everybody who'll listen, why exactly he didn't take part in the Rising. And bragging about all that he did for the Cause for so many years. He never told *me* yet. And if he does. . . .

You're off? Look, take that little poem he sent me this morning. A poem dedicated to Ireland's heroic dead. No, I haven't read it. Nor do I intend to read it. Wait, take the whole row of his slender volumes of poetry. There are poems there that would enchant your senses with their eerie beauty. Take every one of them! Only leave me the bitter memory I hold in my heart for — my Poet, Dark and Slender.

Lead Us Not Into Temptation.

translated by Donall MacAmhlaigh

I

When Alum-ba was king of the land of the Abitines there was a sculptor who was famed throughout the Orient for the excellence of his work. Great kings came from far and wide begging him to carve them yet another statue or image from the hard marble. But he always refused. He wished only to create the great work which his mind had conceived. And to devote himself fully to this work he forsook the great cities and noble houses where a welcome awaited him night and day; he forsook his father and his mother, his brothers and sisters, his companions and his friends; his great fame and fortune, he left them all and he travelled with his old bondsman, until they came to an oakwood close to a quarry of white marble by the banks of a singing stream. There in the oakwood they built two huts, one hut to rest in and one for work. And the two men laboured in the quarry, cutting marble for the great work until the sun went down each day; and in every stone they cut the sculptor saw a portion of the great task on which he had set his heart and he was filled with gladness and exultation that he had turned his back on the follies and the worthless treasures of the world.

The sculptor's heart and soul were devoted to the work he had put before him. He thought of nothing else. The life he had known, cities, diversions, the company of lovely women — they were as nothing compared to his dream. Indeed, almost before he and his old servant had cut and dressed the stones his former life was forgotten.

The noble concept of his mind which was hidden as yet in the marble blocks he began to reveal with hammer and chisel. He worked alone, without respite, in the heart of the leafy wood by the prattling stream from sunrise till sunset; often the sound of his hammer broke the quiet of the oakwood while the birds were still asleep; and then he would lay aside his tools and sit by his work, appraising it . . . . the night birds came out as he sat thus and when he lit his lamp the little winged insects of the woods gathered round his shelter and some would drift through the doorway and it would seem to the sculptor that they were gathered there to give his work acclaim. And they would stay until the old bondsman came with food, the fruits of the forest and water from the spring, and they broke fast together. When they had eaten they would pray together to the gods. They prayed thus —

The sculptor: May the gods give strength to mine arms.
The bondsman: Thy work to do, O Master.
The sculptor: May the gods enlighten my mind.
The bondsman: Thy work to do, O Master.

And the faith and the strength of their words awed the fuzzy little creeping things that invaded their floor, but they would creep back again when the prayers had ended and the two men lay on their beds of dry, brown ferns. They slept on ferns and rushes mainly and often the shadow of his work fell on the face of the sleeping master, but those shadows were never as clear as the project his mind dwelt on even as he slept.

II

One day the great king Alum-ba came to visit the sculptor. The Abitines had conquered their old enemies, the

Partees, and it was thought that the time was ripe to erect a noble temple in honour of the War God in the capital city. And who better to adorn the temple with statues than the sculptor who had retreated to the woods? The king himself and his ministers came to see him. But to no avail. Their entreaties could not move the master.

"Gold nor silver, great houses nor rare foods, fame and power among the people, I crave them not," said the sculptor. "I want only this oakwood to myself, I want only to bring to fruit the dream which my mind has conceived; to shape this hard, white stone . . . . The world is wide; there are other artists who will gladly take up your commissions. Seek them out. Waste not your words on me . . . ." And he went back to his work.

The king sought to coax him by other means. He offered him a great prize, a prize greater than had ever been offered a craftsman before.

"Am I less than the wild mountain ass?" asked the sculptor. "The wild ass may spend his life as he will; he may die of hunger, but he is nobler, if poorer, than his brother who bears the yoke of man. I am a wild mountain ass, O King, and I have no need of great wealth, of fine houses nor servants nor wide acres. Water from the spring, berries from the wood, the light of the sun and my health is all I require . . . . and you are in my light now, O King," and he took up his hammer and chisel again.

But no sooner had the king and his retinue left than others came to visit. Not human folk it was who came this time, but the small winged creatures of the wood, and they hovered round his head, round his work, but the sculptor was unaware of them so lost was he in thought.

III

He worked a whole month, once, striving to shape the form of woman. He was sick, weary, worn and disheartened for he was failing to give expression to the symmetry which he knew lay concealed in the marble. Night came upon him. He lit his lamp and surveyed the work of his hand.

What ailed him that his dream eluded him so? Was it his eye that had failed? It was not. He could see the woman imprisoned in the marble. Was it his hand that had failed him, so? He did not believe that it was; his hand had lost none of its skill.

But he was in torment. He sat on a stool and he remained long in thought, unmoving. His faithful visitors came, the winged insects, the four-legged creepers, the other little creatures of the night. The moon was high and shed a wondrous light. There was a nest of small stars in the eastern sky and the sculptor knew he must get the light of those stars in the eyes of the woman he was shaping.

A shadow fell upon the statue. Some animal from the woods, he thought, had come to his door, blocking the moonlight.

The sculptor raised his head. It wasn't a wood creature . . . . nor yet a woman, he thought, but some creation of the night or the forest, like the other little beings who visited him. But the beauty of the woman (if woman she was) almost robbed him of his senses. Her eyes were luminous stars, stormy night clouds her hair; her form and appearance, the sculptor thought, could exist only in the mind of man. The beauty of the woman made him fearful. If he could but steal some of her loveliness for his work! But she was a fairy woman, not a real one; when the night had passed she would be gone too.

But the first light of day came and she did not go away, but sat there on the ferns regarding him with her shining eyes.

"It is the gods who sent her my way to guide me and to adorn my work and my life," the sculptor said to himself. And he gave thanks a thousand-fold to the gods who had hearkened to his cry, who had helped him in his hour of need.

The woman hidden from him in the hard marble he would soon reveal, now that he had her to help him.

IV

There is a busy trade route between the principal city of the Abitines and Aramana in the land of the Partees. No day of the year but merchants travel this road with their camels and their donkeys and their mules and their wonderful wares. Fine rustling silks from the lands of Arabia; soft, smooth satins from China; precious gems from the wild frozen deserts of the south; embroidery from Persia of the many temples. And the woman saw these treasures borne by the beasts of burden as they went their way and some of them she coveted in her heart.

One day she beheld a large band of merchants coming from the East towards her across the plain as she sat by the wayside pool. The band lingered by the water to let their beasts of burden drink. There was a young merchant in the band and because the woman sitting by the pool was so beautiful he spoke to her. He showed her a jewel. The precious stone he showed her was worth eight hundred Arabian steeds.

"This stone will adorn the crown of a great queen in the Western World," said the merchant. "If I were a rich man," he went on, "I would never part this lovely, noble stone from this lovely, noble woman," and he placed the gem, sparkling, in her rich black hair.

The woman saw the strange light that came to the eyes of the men as they beheld the beauty of the stone and the beauty that was hers; and looking into the clear waters of the pool she knew what it was that made her eyes glow brighter than the jewel which she wore. She resolved that she would have precious stones and fine clothes from then on.

That night she spoke to the sculptor.

"Men not so gifted as you," she said, "can earn wealth; they can give rich garments and precious jewels to their women; could not you do as much for me?"

She spoke those words and others. She coaxed and begged and beguiled him with sweet words, and her soft, sweet voice and her loving looks and with all the wiles that women possess. And since his love for her was seven-fold . . . . he yielded to her.

Within two days it was not the great work beloved of his heart that the master laboured on but a trite little statue that would sell in the city; and when the woman had had her first taste of the sweets of the world she began to go, often, to the city with the statues which she had persuaded the sculptor to carve for her.

Praise is food to the soul of a beautiful woman. She was praised in the city. If she lived in the city poets and musicians and artists would gather round her with songs and poems of praise . . . . but she knew that the master would not readily be prevailed upon to live in the city. What bait could she use to lure him away? The question troubled her greatly, but in the end she knew that she herself must draw him away.

"I shall leave you," she told him one day, "I do not like this wild place. I shall live in the city henceforth," and the false tears welled from her luminous black eyes.

But they did not part. The sculptor forsook the oak-wood; he forsook his old companions, the little winged creatures that came to him by night; he forsook the peace of the woods and they went to the city together.

Pity the man who loves a woman seven-fold!

V

But the great work upon which he had set his heart!

The sculptor continued to work at it but his old zeal had gone. That life was behind him now. A great change had come over him unawares. The follies he had indulged in when he lived in the city before, he indulged in them again now. His love of worldly things returned . . . . and the artist in him withered away though he was still acclaimed by all.

The king came to visit him again but it was not the same man whom he saw in the oakwood that he saw before him now. He had heard that the great task which the master had put before him was almost complete. There was no artist to decorate the great temple which was being built to the God of War: would the master alter his own great work towards that end? He had three days in which to ponder the request, but corrupt as he had become he would not have agreed but for the woman.

She wanted gold to wear.

"Your work is beautiful," she said, "but where could it be better displayed than in a great temple in the capital city of the land? And your work will need but little alteration . . . ."

She did not speak of the rich reward which the king had promised him!

The man yielded to the woman.

The great work was finished at last. It was placed in

the temple but no eye must behold it until the king unveiled it to the throng.

When all was in readiness the sculptor went to the temple alone to see the work of his hand, to gaze on the great work he had set his heart upon, once. His great life's work stood there before him and he stayed throughout the night regarding it and contemplating his life. That great concept which had come to him before he began the labour, he now knew to be unfulfilled. That was very clear to him. He had failed. Why? He let his life pass before him again. He had nobility then, and youth; and he knew only too well how nobility had left him and how baseness had come in its place; he knew that his work had altered as his vision and his soul and his heart had altered . . . .

In the morning came the king and his followers. Came kings from lands afar. The people came and the only name on their lips was the name of the master who gave life to the cold stone; but when the king drew the veil from the great work it was not a stone statue that the kings and the people saw but a statue of flesh . . . .

The sculptor sat on a block there and there was great sorrow and heartbreak and desolation in every line of his form; and the work he had given his heart to, once, lay in fragments about him . . . .

And the woman who had ruined his life and his work . . . . but that's another story.

The Woman in Torment

translated by Diarmuid O Muirithe

A titillating law-case is to be heard before a judge and jury in Galway city next month. Burke of Cnoc Mór and Aindréis Ó Fionnachta from the city are the pair involved, and as judgement shall be given before these words are in print, I think it no harm to tell the tale from beginning to end, precisely as it happened.

One day as Burke, just back from America, was sittting on the idlers' wall in Galway city, he saw coming down the road towards him the most lissom, the most beautifully poised young woman he had ever in his life seen. She wasn't more than eighteen years old, but if you took notice of the footprints she left in the muddy street, you'd swear that they were made by a child of no more than twelve, so small were they.

Burke took a liking to the girl of the tiny feet as she passed by murmuring a song to herself.

He had a small wad of beeswax in his mouth and he spat it out through a gap in his upper teeth down into the water below.

"Who's that young girl?" said he to another idler on the wall.

"Which one?"

"The little lightfooted one."

"A daughter of Aindréis Ó Fionnachta, the shopkeeper who lives near the dock."

"Aindréis Ó Fionnachta?" Burke said twice, ruminatively. "Is he a tall dark man?" he asked suddenly.

135

"That's right."

"With a mole under his right ear?"

"My soul but he has, and a big one too."

"And he's lost the top of his right thumb?"

"You know all about him."

Burke jumped off the wall, picked up his umbrella and set off back the road in a hurry. Over the bridge he went at a brisk pace that he didn't slacken until he arrived at the dock.

Ó Fionnachta was a ship's chandler and Burke paused for a while wondering what he should buy in such a shop. In he went.

"Sixpence worth of mackerel hooks," said he. The man of the house, Ó Fionnachta himself, served him.

"Strange you don't recognise your old friend. You have a bad memory."

The shopkeeper scrutinised him.

"You wouldn't be Séamus a Búrca? You're very like him."

"The very same."

Ó Fionnachta gave him a great welcome. They hadn't seen one another for twenty seven years, since they both worked together in the United States. The stranger was brought into a room at the back of the shop. The two old comrades sat at a table. Glasses were filled and the conversation started. Here's some of it:

"How long is it since we worked together in Panama?" asked the man of the house.

"Twenty seven years, come Christmas."

"You're married, of course?"

"No, I never did marry. Never had time."

"I suppose you've made a power of money, Séamus."

"A little . . . ."

A sailor had come into the shop to buy a few fathoms of rope. The shopkeeper went to the door and told him to make himself at home. He promised not to delay him too long. He filled the two glasses again.

"About yourself," said the stranger, "I hope you don't mind me asking . . . ."

"Not a bit. I'm a widower with a houseful of children. All daughters but for one boy."

"You don't tell me!"

The sailor in the shop was growing impatient. The shopkeeper had to go and serve him. While he was gone Burke started to think about his own predicament. Why should he have to go away again? Hadn't he enough money made? Wouldn't a little comfort be wonderful now after all the years of slaving? And where would he find a nicer place in which to spend the rest of his days than here in the place he was born? When he left the States he had nothing in mind other than a short visit to Ireland, but as the days and months went by the less he felt like returning. The old magical spell! Nostalgia!

When Ó Fionnachta came back from the shop he said to him: "I came back to get married, Aindréis. I'm tired of the life beyond in America."

"One of the Blakes is selling a big farm west of Cnoc Mór, if you know the place. You'd get it for a thousand. He's looking for twelve hundred. A house as fine as ever you saw on it."

"Have you a cart?"

"I have."

"Tackle the horse straight away and let's go look at it."

While the horse was being tackled the following conversation took place: "You've a bad memory, Aindréis," said Burke, "if you don't remember that Christmas night long ago when we promised each other that one of us would never be short of a wife as long as the other had a daughter on his hands."

"I remember it well, and I'll keep my end of the bargain if what you tell me about your money is true."

"If herself is willing . . . ."

"Why wouldn't she be?"

"There are great women going nowadays. Look at them over in England. There's no stopping them!"

Before the cart arrived the two men had made the match. A few nights later Máire Ní Fhionnachta and her father were together. He told her about the match. She was dissatisfied with it. She said she'd never marry him. He told her she would. She assured him she wouldn't . . . . But she did.

It is no lie to say that they had a lovely house at Cnoc Mór and that they lived accordingly. The house had originally been built for some nobleman or other who, in the course of time, lost all he had and was forced to sell. Of course, everybody thought that Ó Fionnachta's daughter had made a great match. The best day they ever had, what had they? And if her man wasn't exactly in the springtime of his life, few people would guess that he was moving on towards fifty. Was there a young fellow in the parish of Cnoc Mór who could do a day's work like him? Where was the man who had the same drive in him? Wouldn't it do your heart good to see him working? And God knows he was fond of her! The mean little thing without health or strength or spirit!

They were right. He had the strength. He was a worker; and he was very fond of that little woman he married.

But she was far from happy. That strange love he had for her was the cause of her trouble. He was uncouth. Life across the water was the cause of it, perhaps: the hard times and the slavery and all he saw there . . . . Be that as may be, she would shiver a little every time he came near her for fear he might become too amorous. She could feel the iciness under her skin whenever he laid a hand on her.

Not that she would admit to any of this. She thought it a great sin; nevertheless she felt greatly relieved whenever he told her that he was off to this fair or that, and that he wouldn't be back for a few days. She just couldn't help it. If she were to lose this world and the next on account of it, she couldn't give him that love a woman gives a man; and as soon as he had left her she wondered about her friends and asked herself if many of them were in the same plight as she was.

He never knew how she felt. He was shrewd and intelligent, a good man to strike a bargain or to unravel the mysteries of business and politics; but he could never understand people who were not cast in the same rough mould as he was. What was the cause of it all? The kind of life he had led in America, the misery, the slavery, the great desire to make money? Or was it some demon he had inherited from his ancestors?

Sometimes when his wife was moody or peevish he would attempt to placate her, but his words of consolation always seemed to her to be coarse and vulgar and they disgusted her. He had often noticed this loathing and he could never understand it. He had never met a woman like her; every woman he had ever met in America could be placated with flattery and coaxed with presents.

He came to the conclusion that he should give his wife a beautiful gift in the hope that she would change her strange ways. He went to Galway to buy the gift. He saw what all the shops had to offer and he finally decided on a splendid, fashionable silk gown. Not satisfied with that, he bought a big gold brooch for her bosom. He had always been most generous towards her and had been perfectly extravagant on this occasion; but what harm — wouldn't she be happy when she saw them!

And she was happy. She had never seen a nicer gown. Such a beautiful cut! When her husband held it out for her to inspect she could have sworn that no woman, no matter how slim, could wear it. She took the dress to try it on.

"I'm very grateful to you, Séamus. I really am very grateful."

She put it on. It was a very tight fit indeed and he said so.

"But that's the way I like it, Séamus. I'll be the height of fashion."

"In a few months time, you won't be able to get into it at all . . . ." He said much more that won't be related here—things his wife loathed him for saying. And when he refused to hold his tongue she started to cry and ran into the bedroom.

He regretted saying such things to her; he should have realized she resented that kind of talk, so he knocked on the door, hoping to offer some sort of apology. But she refused to let him in.

"Open the door," he said.

"I will not," she replied.

He was getting very angry.

"The further you stay away from me the more I like it," she said.

She opened the door slightly and threw the dress out.

"The next time you feel like buying a present, buy it for somebody else."

He was furious. He waited a minute or two at the door, undecided as to what to do. He felt like breaking it down with his shoulder and teaching her a lesson she'd never forget. But he didn't do so. Instead, he picked up the lovely gown and threw it into the fire.

"To hell with her," he said, "but I'll teach her manners!"

He left the house, mounted his white horse and rode her to the centre of Galway. He was seen on the road that night and never have people heard such foul language; never have they seen a horse being so badly treated.

The male child his wife gave birth to never saw the light of day. Two doctors from Galway attended her at the birth. The baby was stillborn and they warned that in their opinion the mother's life would be at risk if ever she had another child.

When the woman recovered her husband paid no attention to her. About this time he started to travel from fair to fair buying cattle to fatten on his farm at Cnoc Mór. Quite often his wife would neither see him nor hear from him for a week, but she did not care. Even when he was at home they rarely spoke to one another. He would get up in the morning, eat his meal and go out to see to the cattle, and she would not see him again till dinner-time; almost every night he had the company of local men in the kitchen, and they often spent a good part of the night playing cards and carousing. He always drank heavily, but he was as strong as a bullock and it did not seem to do him any harm. Yet little by little the dissipation took its toll, and quite often he did not get to bed before dawn. He would sometimes refuse to speak to his wife for days at a time, and the long silence was broken only to inquire whether she had done this or that, or whether she needed some money for housekeeping.

She had an idea that he no longer had any respect for her, and where there is no respect there is no love. She was quite content with matters as they were. As long as he didn't bother her she was contented, or almost so. It was a hard life, she thought, to be married to a man she hated, but what could she do?

He owned every acre of the land he farmed and it wasn't until he came home drunk from Galway one night that his wife found out what was troubling him.

"He won't get it, whoever gets it," he said to himself as he sat by the fire while she was preparing a meal for him.

"He won't get it, the bastun, the thieving scoundrel,

the cursed rogue," he mumbled, ignoring his wife. She soon knew what he meant.

"He knows that there are none of my people left . . . . but he won't get it and neither will anyone belonging to him . . . . I'd rather sell the land and throw the money into the sea."

He lifted his head and saw his wife. It was near the dawn and she had got up in case he should kill himself on the stone flags of the yard. Should he be killed far from home without her knowing, she wouldn't be too sorry about it but at any rate when he lifted his head she thought that she had never seen, and she hoped that she would never again see, a face as ugly as the face she looked at. She was about to leave him there and go to her own room but he uttered some obscenity and caught her by the shoulder.

She managed to escape from him because he was very drunk, but he fell and lay on the cold flags until the sun rose.

*

He rode the white horse from fair to fair and from town to town by this time, and horse and rider were often seen on the roads at midnight, the rider in a drunken stupor relying on the horse to get him safely to his destination. The rider's wife was at home, and whenever she expected him she spent a sleepless night waiting. It wasn't through love for him that she used to sit at the window until she heard the hoof beats on the road, hoping that she would never again hear them, but that the horse's rider would have a drink too many and be thrown head first on to the road.

The things she thought of! She used to see her husband being brought home at dawn stone dead. The neighbours coming in saying how sorry they were that she had los a good man. She wondered what she should say to them and whether or not she could keen for him.

But she was a pious devout woman and although these things entered her head, she didn't dwell on them.

She used to hear the horse cantering on the road a long way off and she would listen carefully for her husband's voice so as to know what state he was in; she always knew how drunk he was from his voice, and the drunker he was the more she feared him. When he came in merry and was amorous in his own rough way she used to try to escape from him. She rarely succeeded. How she hated him! How she loathed him when she felt his heavy drunken breath on her cheek . . . .

She was a timorous little thing by nature and she would never have done anything but for something he said to her one day at breakfast. He told her that he despised her, that he couldn't have any regard for such a woman—she had left him without an heir.

He said many other things that hurt her before he left the house. She watched him going back the road on the white horse and she prayed to God that he would never return.

So she waited at the window that night wondering would she hear the horse. She didn't. Midnight came, one o'clock, two, three, and still no horse. She had plenty of time to think of the life she led but it was what her husband said to her that morning and the way in which he said it that annoyed her most. It was a moonlit night and she decided to go outside. Almost immediately she decided never to return.

She pulled her cloak around her and walked through the night all the way to Galway. She was by her father's hearth before daybreak.

Three days later Burke followed her to the city. Ó Fionnachta himself greeted him, and he was brought into the room at the back of the shop. As always, a glass was filled for him.

"This is a nasty business," said Ó Fionnachta.

"She's to blame," said Burke.

Her father had only heard part of the story. The young woman was too ashamed to tell him the worst of it and even if she had done so he probably would not have understood it fully. He put the whole thing down to the follies and the quirks of youth and he thought that he could settle the matter easily. He advised her to go back to her husband but she refused. That of course was but the foolish talk of a young woman. Still, he would have to teach her husband a lesson; he would have to frighten him. For too long he had been drinking too much and rambling too much.

"I suppose you have come for her," said Ó Fionnachta.

"She's here then?"

He suspected she wasn't.

"Where else would she be? And here she'll stay or so she says."

"No she won't. I'm her husband."

Burke was arrogant. He thought he had right on his side.

"Too much drink and carousing you've had for this past year," said Ó Fionnachta. "A drop now and again never did a man any harm, but every night of the year . . . Wherever you go all you'll hear is 'Did you hear what Burke from Cnoc Mór did lately?' or 'Isn't he a great man for the drink?' It's scandalous, man! Scandalous!"

"I don't give a rambling damn what they say: my business is my own. Where's Máire?"

"Your business is your own surely, but I have a daughter married to you."

"If they don't know the truth they'll tell the lie."

"And the truth is bad enough!"

"Aye," said Burke, lamely as he attempted to guess how much of the truth his old friend had been told.

"Make your peace in the name of God," said Ó Fionnachta, "and don't have the countryside laughing at us. I'll call herself."

He did so. She came bustling in. She nodded to the two men and said: "If you've come for me, Seamus, you've made a journey for nothing."

"You must come with me. I'm your husband."

"Wouldn't you take a little advice," said her father. "Wise as you are you still have some sense to learn."

"If I had the slightest bit of sense I wouldn't have given into you both in the beginning, but I bought my sense since then, and I bought it dearly, and you both know that I had a hard master."

She went on and on. The two men were astonished at her boldness.

"To go back to that fine house at Cnoc Mór and to stay there with that man there who used to insult me every day of the year and is so blind that he wouldn't even know when he was insulting me. A man who never wanted anything else but to satisfy his own lust . . . ."

Her father tried to stop her. He hadn't known that things were so bad; had he known, he might not have told her to go back.

But she wasn't ashamed anymore nor was she afraid. She would say what was in her mind no matter what would come of it. The two men stood at either side of the table and she stood at its head and she was so agitated that she had to grip a chair from time to time for support.

"I'd much rather to spend my life and my health begging for my bread than to spend even one night under the same roof with you Seamus Burke."

Her father spoke timidly. He had become slightly shy in her presence.

"And I'm not too thankful to you either," said she.

"All you wanted was to get a man for me and you didn't give a damn what sort of a man he was so long as he had a little money. To sell me—that's all you wanted. There are men in it and God shouldn't give them daughters; there's another crowd and the great sin is that they get women . . . ."

"Close your mouth, woman. Close your mouth, I say," said Burke, threatening. "I have only one word to say: You're my wife and where I'll be you'll be and if you don't come home with me willingly you'll come home another way . . . ."

He tried to grab her. Ó Fionnachta came between them. It looked for a moment as if there would be a fight.

"You might as well go home tonight, Burke," said the father. "This business won't be settled that way."

He went home. That night two men, one in Galway city and the other in Cnoc Mór, thought for a long time about the character of women.

A week later Burke was very surprised to get a letter from his wife saying that she would be willing to go home with him. She asked him to come and collect her.

He did so. As his cart passed the Teach Bán Burke decided to ask her why she gave in. He was delighted that he had succeeded in breaking her spirit.

"There was no point in tormenting yourself," he said. "Didn't you know you'd have to come back? I suppose your father told you he couldn't keep you any longer and him with such a big family to look after."

"That's not the reason I'm here in this cart with you now," she replied. "He'd give me the bit out of his mouth."

"Why else would you give in like this?"

"A word in your ear."

She whispered something to him, told him her secret. Night was falling. the old white horse was plodding along on a free rein. No birds sang. The couple heard nothing but the noise the horse and trap made on the road.

What she had said had silenced them both. Burke looked at her. She looked dolefully ahead, her hand resting limply on the frame of the trap. He laid his hand on hers and started to caress it tenderly, hoping she wouldn't be repelled by what he was doing. She wasn't.

"Máire . . . . Máire," he said, but another word he wasn't able to utter.

Her baby was a boy and she died having him.

A little while afterwards a young man walking the road near Cnoc Mór heard a cart coming behind him. It was Burke's cart and as the young man knew both the woman who had died and her father, he gave him a lift. Burke was in a talkative mood and his companion had no option but to listen.

"He'll pay dearly for saying I killed her. And the way I loved her! But there's a law in the land, and I'll show him he can't call me a murderer!"

They were passing the churchyard of Cnoc Mór.

"She's buried in there. That's her grave."

He stopped the white horse.

"We might as well go in and say a prayer for her."

The two men knelt at the graveside. When they had said their prayer Burke said: "I thank you, God, for not laying your hand too heavily on me, because if you took away the woman I loved since I first laid eyes on her, she has given me an heir . . . ."

The other man could stand it no longer. In a frenzy of anger he faced Burke.

"You bloody bastard! It's a good job for you that it's over the grave of this woman we stand . . . . the woman I myself have loved for years. But for that . . . ."

Suddenly he turned and left the churchyard for fear he'd strangle the wretched man who had destroyed the love of his young life.

Knitting

translated by Thomas Murphy

I'm down and my heart is heavy throughout the day, and it's not without reason.

And yesterday I was laughing with the springtime of the year, and life laughing along with me, as I travelled the sea-shore from dawn to dusk. But today is a different story and I cannot lift myself out of its gloom.

At the fall of night, last night, I went to the house of a couple that were very great with me one time but, life being what it is, I hadn't had tide or tidings of them for ten years. But they would be the one to have the welcome for me, and wouldn't we have the great stories to exchange! I began to think, gathering my best and strangest adventures so as to set the pair of them laughing. And I'd have the right stories for the children too . . . . Yes, how many of them were in it? They had three sons ten years ago; they'd be fine tall boys by now, and maybe the house filled with other children as well. But, for the life of me, if I could remember the names of the three sons. I'd be ashamed of that.

No matter, my spirits were soaring, going to become re-acquainted with my old friends.

The man was in the parlour when I was let in and, though it was only dusk, he had the lamp lit on the table and the same with the candles in the windows. It struck me at first sight that he was looking worn, and older than his years. Somehow life had weighed heavily upon him. And he a fine tall man only into his middle years.

But the biggest wonder of all was what he was doing. There were gloves and mittens and all classes of garments on the table before him; they were knitted from the finest silken thread. And the business that was occupying my friend so earnestly was unravelling the knitted garments and winding up the thread again.

You'd know that he felt ashamed at being discovered in such work, for no sooner did he see me but he threw it from him in a way as if to hide the matter, and then he welcomed me in his own generous manner. I was curious to ask what had him so occupied but the question would embarrass him.

"Here is a man," I said to myself, "suffering the pains of hell."

*

After a while I asked how was his wife. He seemed reluctant to reply but kept silent, looking into the fire as one in lingering thought.

I let the matter rest. Some disagreement or falling-out that was between them, I thought, and he didn't want to talk about it. That was a pity, because if there was a man in Ireland had the love and affection for his wife, that man was my friend. But isn't that the way with the story always, there's no cure for love but marriage.

And the fondness they had for each other ten years ago!

We talked about the world. It's hard to become reacquainted with a person after ten years.

"And the family," I said, "are ye all well?"

He sighed.

"May the Son of God help me," he said pitifully, "but I'll have to tell you the whole story."

He prepared himself, making ready to talk, but no sooner was he started than the door opened and who came in but his wife.

I stood up to greet her but she walked past me without as much as a glance. Indeed, she didn't even raise her eyes, but she knitting away earnestly the whole while. And wasn't I in great wonder to see that it was a silken shawl she was knitting, and wasn't it a silken shawl that her husband was unravelling!

The man had stood up too. He greeted her in his princely manner but she paid no more attention to him than she did to myself.

He arranged the big cosy chair in front of the fire. He couldn't have been more attentive if it was out of a sick bed she was after getting. And there was no colour or resemblance of sickness about her. On the contrary, she looked the picture of health, tall and stately, with a black dress of silk on her. She was past the forty mark but you wouldn't take her for much more than thirty.

She remained standing, her eyes cast down, still knitting away, until he took her arm gently and seated her. It wasn't because of anything between them or any falling-out that had made him reluctant to talk about her earlier: it was plain to see—it would be clear to the blind—that he was as fond of her now as he was in his youth.

But what was the matter with her? What sense could there be in this eternal knitting, and to be heedless of all else?

The place and the silent pair of them in the room were beginning to unsettle and weigh on me. If someone spoke it would have eased me and scattered the gloom that was in it. But no word was spoken since the woman had entered, and there was nothing to be heard but the sound of the knitting-needles knocking one against the other, and the occasional sigh from the man sitting beside me, his head bowed in sorrow.

Now and again the knitting fell to the floor; but in no way did this upset her. She went on with her labour, working her fingers as if she was still holding the needles in her hands. And when the sound of the needles was not to be heard the man would know what had happened, and he'd stoop and hand the knitting back to her without a word being spoken. And though more often than not his head was bowed, there was hardly a stir from her that he'd miss, and his only care was to assist her in every way he could.

Hadn't I the pity for them when I realised that the gentle graceful woman he had given his heart to was gone clean out of her mind!

*

But that knitting, and the click-click of the needles knocking one against the other! And the sighs escaping from the man when his thoughts descended to scald the heart of him.

After a long time (long years they seemed to me) the knitting stopped and the woman craned her neck, listening.

"Is that Seán calling me?" she said.

"I expect it is," said the man.

I wondered at them hearing a call for I heard no sound. The woman stood up.

"I think the poor creature has a cold," she said. "The world itself wouldn't keep him out of the puddles."

She went to the door, the knitting in her hands. The man arose and opened the door as you would for a queen.

"That's the way she is this two years," he said, returning to the fire. "Her mind and sense are gone clean from her."

What good seeking to offer condolences on such an occasion!

I recalled that Seán was the eldest son and to make conversation I said, "But I didn't hear him call."

"My regret and misfortune that you didn't," said he.

He looked at me.

"But did you not hear of the great sorrow that blighted the life in this house on us?"

I said I hadn't heard.

"It was a fine day at the end of spring two years ago that my heart was broken." The poor man had a catch in his throat. He was silent a nice while. "That day my three sons went out in an old boat . . . . the boat was leaking . . . . the three of them were drowned . . . . it was myself that brought the bodies ashore . . . .

"And my beautiful Sinéad is without mind or reason since. In her own strange way she thinks the three of them are still with us in the house, and she's forever knitting for them . . . . but for myself unravelling what she does from time to time, the house would be filled with mittens and gloves . . . ."

We were silent for a long while. Then I arose and took hold of his hand; we looked into each other's eyes and he understood the sympathy I had for him and for his handsome stately wife on whom God had laid a heavy hand.

Nora, daughter of Marcus Beag

translated by Thomas McCarthy

I

You never saw such surprise as that of the people of Ros Dha Loch when they heard that Nora, daughter of Marcus Beag, was to go to England. A sister of hers was already over there, working, but Nora was needed at home. There would be nobody left after her except the old couple. The two brothers she had never did any good — for themselves or for anyone belonging to them. Martin, the eldest one, was sent to Galway to be a shop-boy, (old Marcus always had notions), but he wasn't long there when he lost his job because of the drink and after that he joined the British Army. As for Stephen, the second one, there was no stopping the old fellow from thinking that he would make a "gentleman" of him, but when the headstrong lad didn't get his own way from the father he stole off with the price of two bullocks sold at Uachtarard fair in his pocket.

"He's no better here than out of here," the old man said on hearing that he was gone. But he was only pretending that the story didn't hurt him. Often at night he was unable to sleep a wink thinking about the two sons who had left him and gone astray. With any one of the neighbours who would try to brighten the dark old man then, as to sympathise with him over the misfortune of his sons, he would say nothing except—"What's the good in talking? Very little thanks I got for trying to keep them in the old nest. The two of them took flight and left me by myself. They'll give me little cause for worry from now on."

But they did. And up until Nora said that she had decided not to stay at home any longer nothing troubled him but the way the two sons had left him. He had been shamed by them. People were making fun of him. He was the laughing stock of the village—himself and his family. And the way that he'd thought that he'd give them a decent livelihood. The way he worked himself to the bone, labouring morning to dusk in all weathers to keep them at school until they might be as erudite as the master himself, indeed!

But it would be a different story with Nora, according to himself. He would keep her at home. He would find a match for her. He would leave the small-holding to herself and her husband after death. When she told him that she would leave he thought that she was just joking. But it was soon clear to him that she wasn't. Then he did his level best to keep her at home. It was useless. It was no use his wife talking to her either. For a month there was great antagonism between them: the old man threatening every evil on her head if she left, herself trying to better him. But her mind was set on going, and across she'd go no matter what was said.

"You had two sons," she said to him one night, "and they left you. The two of them showed you. You don't know that I wouldn't do the same, if you don't leave me go willingly."

"She's the last of them, Marcus," said the wife, "and by God I hate to part with her at the end of my life, but," she continued and she nearly weeping, "maybe 'tis for her own good."

The father didn't think so. He was adamant. He was certain that it was far far better for her to stay where she was and make a match there. Her husband would have forty acres of land when her old father died. She was a pleasant and affectionate girl. There wasn't a farmer or shop-keeper in the seven parishes which were nearest to them who wouldn't be very happy to marry her.

"And why wouldn't they be," he said, "such a lovely girl and with forty acres of land."

But he had to give in in the end.

It's then they saw the work! The great vexation and anxiety that had come over Nora for a while was all gone, apparently. There wasn't a trace to be seen. She was as light and festive as the best days of her life, or so it seemed. They had so many things to do. Hats and dresses to make and decorate. Cloth and ribbons of every kind to be bought and dyed. She hadn't one break in the weeks before she went. Visiting here today and elsewhere tomorrow.

She didn't shed one tear until the two big travelling boxes that she had bought in Galway were put on the cart that was to take them to the railway station at Ballinahinch. Then she wept profusely. When they were east at the crossroads the showers of tears were on the cheeks.

"May God have mercy on them," said one of the boys who was thrown on a ditch that was on a smooth mossy patch by the roadside.

"Amen," said another one of them, "and everyone like them."

"But do you know what's the matter with her that she's going away?"

"It wouldn't surprise me in the least if she could do well at home."

"Three fellows came asking for her last year—the three of them well known for their money."

"It's said that she had great time for the son of Sean Matthew, the shop-keeper," said the old man in their midst.

"The one who was at the big college in Galway?"

"The very one."

"I don't believe it. He was a bad lad."

"You don't say."

The cart was moving northwards through the great flat bogland between Ross and Ballinahinch. Nora could still see her own house below in the glen. It wasn't about that she was thinking, but on the misfortunate day that the son of Sean Matthew met her at the Ros Dha Loch crossroads, and he spending his holidays at his uncle's house in the village eastwards. She didn't stop thinking about that until she reached Ballinahinch. The train let off a sharp impatient whistle as if it was telling people to hurry up and not delay something so huge and lively and powerful. Nora went in. The train gave a little jolt. It started to move slowly. Marcus Beag walked by its side. He took leave of his daughter and returned home sad and sorrowful.

II

It was true for the wise old man who was thrown on the mossy green looking at life and letting it go by that she once gave her heart to the son of Sean Matthew at one point in her life. But that time was gone. And it wouldn't be a lie to say that it was an angry and intense hatred that she had for the fine young man who was over in Glasgow in a college studying to be a doctor. Because of that love that she had had for him she now had to leave

Ros Dha Loch and her closest friends and bring the burden of the world on herself. He had been her most beloved once, that bright young man who spent his holidays in Ros Dha Loch, more so than any other person she'd ever met. And weren't those wonderful stories that he told her about the life they'd have in the great towns out foreign! And how his tales pleased her! And when he said to the foolish naive girl that he'd never met anyone he loved more than her, how pleased and heart-warmed she'd been! And the wonderful house that they'd have when he'd be a doctor!

And she believed everything that the young fellow told her. He believed it himself—while he was saying it. Indeed, such foolish talk didn't worry him too much when he went away. But it was different with Nora. It would be a long time before he'd come back again. Summertime was a long way away! 'Twould be a long time before it would be summer always.

She had had great trust but she was deceived. The letters she sent him were returned to her. He was in another place. Nobody had any information on him. Her life was confused. Her mind was in a turmoil when she understood the story correctly. She was thinking about him and turning it all over in her mind by day and by night. She could do nothing but leave the place entirely. She, herself, and everyone associated with her were ashamed in front of people. A young girl who used to be a servant in Ros Dha Loch was working over in London. She would head for that city. She would make for that city now and not for the big town where her sister was.

Sitting in the train she was filled with wonder at the way rivers and harbours, lake, mountain and plain flew past while she herself did nothing. Why were they all moving away from her? What kind of life would be there for her in the foreign faraway land where this wonderful vehicle would leave her? Dread and trembling came over her. Darkness was falling on the flatland and the mountains. A halt was put to her thoughts but it was clear to her that she was borne away on some strange animal; until she felt her heart starting and jumping with the force of anger; until she was a fire-dragon, and flames leaping from her eyes; that she was being taken to some terrible wasteland—a place where there was neither sunshine nor rainfall; that she had to go there against her will; that she was being banished to this wasteland because of one sin.

The train reached Dublin. She felt that the whole place was disturbed by a great single drone of sound. Men screaming and shouting. Trains coming and going and blowing whistles. The noise of men, of trains, of carriages. Everything she saw filled her with wonder. The boats and shipping on the Liffey. The bridges, the streets that were lit up at midnight. The people, the city itself that was so beautiful, so full of life, so bright in those dead hours of the night. For a little while she nearly forgot the misfortune that drove her from her own hometown.

But when she was on the train over, the reverse was true. The terrible dark thoughts pressed down on her again. There was no stopping them. Why did she leave her home anyway? Wouldn't it have been better to stay, no matter what happened to her? What would she do now? What was going to happen to her in the place where she was going?

Things like that. If there were people long ago who spent a hundred years to discover that life was but a day, as the old storytellers tell us, she herself did something more marvellous. She made a hundred years out of one single day. She became old and withered in just one day. Every sorrow and heartbreak, and every great trouble of the mind that comes upon a person over a lifetime came to her in one single day from the time she left Ros Dha Loch to the moment she was at the centre of London, England—the moment she saw Kate Ryan, the servant girl they had had at home, waiting for her at the side of the train to give welcome. She never understood life until that very day.

III

The two young women were living in a miserable ugly back street on the southside of the city. In a large sprawling house where the people were on top of each other in one great heap was where they lived at that time. You never saw the likes of Nora's amazement when she saw the number of them that were there. She could have sworn that there was at least one hundred people, between men, women and children. She used to be left alone there for the whole day, because Kate had to go out to work from morning until dusk. She would sit at the window looking at all the people going by, wondering where they could all be going. She wasn't long like that until she began to wonder if she's made a mistake in coming at all. She wondered why she had left the lonely village in the west among the hills on the edge of the great ocean. What would her father say if he knew why? He'd be furious of course.

"Why had I the misfortune more than anyone else?" she would say. But that was too insoluble a question, and when she couldn't find an answer she'd go out onto the street; but she wouldn't go far for fear of getting lost. But the same thoughts pressed down on her in the street among people, just like in the house.

One night, when Kate came home from work, Nora was sitting by the fire crying.

"Now, now, Nora love," she said, "dry your eyes and drink a cup of tea with me. I was told to tell you that a girl is needed by relatives of my mistress, and if you would go there . . . ."

"I'll go there," Nora said, rising quickly.

On the following morning she journeyed to the house of the lady. She started work there. She had so much to do there, so many new thoughts entered her mind, that she couldn't think of anything else for a little while. In the letters she sent home she included a little money even thought she knew that they didn't lack much because they were already well set up. And the letters her father sent to her, she used to read and reread every night before going to bed. They used to have news of the village. That the fishermen had had a great catch of herring. That Tomas Pats Mor had bought a new boat. That Nell Griffin had emigrated to America.

A few months went like that but in the end the lady told her that she wasn't satisfied with her and that she'd have to leave. She had to do that. She left what she had behind her and went. She had no shelter or protection that night but the rain falling on her and the hard streets under her feet.

Is it necessary to talk about everything that happened to her after that? About the "young nobleman" who gave her food and drink and money and she at the end of her tether with want and need. About the way that she started on the drink. About the way she tried to deceive herself, and daze and blind her mind. About the different people who met her in houses of drink and otherwise. About their talk and their conversation. About the way her self-esteem was narrowed until after a while she didn't care what might become of her. About the way she was going to the bad day by day, until in the end she had no care or honour, but walked the streets.

IV

Nine years she had like that. Drinking and carousing at night. Dressing up and getting herself ready during the day for the next night. Any thought that used to come into her head about the life she lived now and the one she lived at home she banished as quickly as she could. It was thoughts like that that caused her most unease. And—even if it's true that a person would have no interest whatsoever in living unless he thought that somehow he was doing more good than bad—she couldn't do any differently. But those thoughts came mercilessly against her will in their hundreds and hundreds during the day—especially after she had just sent a letter home, a thing she often did. And when they came upon her thickly like that she would go out drinking.

She was out one night walking the streets after she had just sent a letter home that contained some money. It was eleven o'clock. The people were coming out of the theatres in their thousands and thousands and she looking at them. There were some among them who stared at her and at women of her kind. The kind of look that shows the desire and greed which brings destruction on people, that drives countries against each other and which gave material to poets and storytellers of the world from the time of Troy to the present day.

She wasn't long like that when she saw a man in front of her, his woman by his side. They stared at each other, without knowing why. They recognised each other. It was the son of Sean Matthew who was a doctor in London. She turned on her heels quickly. She heard him say it to his wife on going into a restaurant that was near them, and that he would join her shortly. Nora moved off on hearing that. He was after her. She quickened her walk. He did the same. She was trotting, he trotting after her. She had a head start on him. She ran up one street and down another. She feeling that he was at her heels. She worried to death that he might catch her. That everyone would find out about her predicament at home. That everyone would know.

A chapel was just in front of her—a small chapel that stayed open all night because of some feast day. She needed the shelter there from the man who was after her—that man to whom she gave the love in her heart and who'd deceived her. She had no recollection of getting inside, but in she went. What she saw made her feel strange, it had been so long since she was inside a church. Her youth came back to her. She was in Ros Dha Loch Church again. A statue of the Blessed Virgin was in a corner and a red light in front of it. She made for that corner. She threw her hands around it. She was shaking and rocking back and forth with heaviness of mind. Her bright peaked hat almost falling off her head. Her bright red ribbons drenched and soiled by the mud of the street. She was praying to God and the Virgin out loud, prayer after prayer, until she exclaimed in a strong fervent voice: "Holy Mary — Mother of God — pray for us sinners now and at the hour of our death — Amen!"

An old priest behind her heard her pray. He spoke to her in a kind gentle manner. He calmed her. He took her with him. He questioned her. She told him her story without holding anything back. She showed him the letters she had received from her father.

He put further questions to her.

Yes—she was satisfied going home. 'Twas she who sent the money home with which the old man bought the fishing boat. She was certain that they didn't — they didn't know anything about the life she led in London.

"And did your father ask you why you didn't go to your sister in the first place?"

"He did. But I told him that the work was better in London."

They spent a good while like that—himself questioning and she giving the answers. He found decent lodging for her for the night. He told her to send a letter home to say that she was thinking of returning, and that he would visit her the following day and that she would be able to make a confession. That night before he went to sleep he wrote a long letter to the Parish Priest of Ros Dha Loch telling him the story and asking him to keep an eye on the young woman when she arrived home.

They were expecting her at home. Everybody was saying that no person ever left Ros Dha Loch who did as well as her. There was no one among them who had sent that kind of money home.

"It must give you great satisfaction, Marcus," Sean the Blacksmith was saying and he putting a shoe on Marcus' horse down in the forge on the day she was coming home, "that in the end she's coming home, because you haven't got anybody to leave the land to."

"Well you may say it," he replied, "and I'm a fair old age an' all."

The horse and cart was fitted out for his journey to the railway station for her.

"They used to say," he said boastfully and he fixing the horse to the cart, "that the other two did nothing, which was true I suppose, but you wouldn't believe the help she gave me. Look at the big fishing boat that'll be chasing mackerel tonight—I couldn't have bought it but for her."

"You're saying nothing but the truth now, Marcus," said the old man who was giving him a hand, "but tell me this," he said nervously: "Did she ever tell you that my Seamus met her in some place?"

"I did ask her that, but she never saw him."

"Well, look at that now. . . . And I haven't had a letter from him in six months."

Marcus left. He hadn't been so light-hearted for many a long day as he went off to the railway station. If his sons had gone to the bad his daughter had surpassed all. She was an example for the whole parish. Now they wouldn't be able to say that he'd have to sell the land in the end. He would keep Nora at home. He would make a match for her. He would find her a solid, prudent man. . . .

These thoughts hadn't ended when the train came in majestically. Nora came off it. And he had some welcome for her! And even greater than his, if that was possible, was the welcome that her mother gave her at home.

But didn't she look spent and tired! What did they do to her at all? Was it the way she'd been doing too much work? But she wouldn't be at home long before she would have a good appearance again. The wan cheeks would be gone; if she stayed at home and took their advice.

"And the first bit of advice I'll give you is to have this lovely bit of meat and cabbage, because I suppose you never had time to have a bit to eat in that city," said the old woman and she laughing.

But Nora couldn't eat. She wasn't a bit hungry. She was too upset from the long journey, she said. She would go straight to the room and undress. She would rest there. And after a while maybe she'd be able to eat something.

"Or maybe you'd like a cup of tea to begin with," her mother said when she was back in the room.

"I'd prefer that," she said, "maybe it would do me some good."

That night when the people of the town came in to

welcome her they couldn't see her. They were told that she was so exhausted from the journey that she had to go asleep, but that they would see her tomorrow. Nora heard their talk and conversation as she was across in her room praying to God and The Virgin to put her on the right road from now on and to give her the power to stay that way forever.

V

It was amazing the way Nora worked after her homecoming. Within the person who was called Nora Marcus Beag in Ros Dha Loch there were two actual women: the young gentle one who had spent some time in England earning money and another woman who remained unknown to the people of the village, but who had suffered the hardships of life in a foreign city. And just as there were two persons, you might say, there were two minds and two modes of thought there as well. She had the outlook of the woman who had been led astray in London as well as the viewpoint she had before she ever left her native place at all.

And she bore the constant conflict between them. The woman who had once led a wild life fighting with the other woman who never left and who wanted nothing except to stay at home, settled and secure. It was a hard struggle. Sometimes the evil was stronger, she'd think, and then she could be seen making for the Chapel. And all the people saying that they'd never seen a young woman so devout and pious and polite as herself.

During this time the village nearest to them had a pattern-day. A large number of people from Ros went there. Some of them walking, some riding, and some others across the harbour in their boats. Some of them went there to sell stock. Yet others had no particular business there.

Nora was one of this crowd. She was walking around the fair looking at the cattle that were being sold. Getting to know people here and enquiring after some person who had left the district since she first left for London. She was cheery, all dressed-up and upright. A dress of the best white cotton, the most expensive, was what she wore. A dress that she'd brought back from London. Fine satin ribbons trailing after her. Peacock feathers standing up in her hat. She hadn't been so breezy and happy for a long time. It was a terribly hot day. The sun was glaring down ferociously. If it wasn't for the little breeze that came in off the harbour now and again, one couldn't take the heat. Nora was exhausted by the day. She heard violin music close by. Soft, sweet, pleasant music. The fiddler was sitting by the door of the cabin. His head swaying back and forth. Such a satisfied and contented expression on his face and in his manner that you'd think he'd never had any worry or trouble in his life before and never would.

Nora went in. She sat on a stool by the door to listen to the music. She was exhausted. If she could only have a drink! That's what she thought. That conflict was started again. She was just about to leave when a young man from Ros came over to her to ask if she'd have a glass with him.

"The day itself is so hot that it wouldn't do a bit of harm to you. Have anything you like."

She took a glass from him.

Any person who's been fond of the drink at a point in their life and who's stayed off it for a while, and who again touches a drop, 'tis certain that he'll drink a second glass, and a third one, and maybe a ninth one, because the old desire is reawakened.

That was the way it was with Nora. She drank the second one. And the third one. It soon went to her head. She began to make a show. She went out and danced. But she had to give up before long. Dizziness was in her head. Her legs had gone from under her. She was barely able to go out but she hadn't got far when she fell on a bank by the side of the road.

A few hours of night had gone by when her father found her like that.

He lifted her into the cart and drove her home.

The following morning the same cart was being prepared outside the door.

"If those are the kind of tricks you learned in England," he said and bitterness in his voice, "it's there you can be practising them."

The two of them went to the railway station.

The very night that Nora left you could see an old man inside a fishing boat if you were by Ros Dha Loch shore. A container was drawn up by his side and he trying to obliterate the name that was written on the boat. Even if he did, he didn't succeed in rubbing the name from his heart. 'Twas the name of his daughter that was on the boat.

Nell

translated by John Jordan

The only light in the room came from a street lamp
standing at the corner of the house, but nonetheless there
was a woman there, watering the plants in boxes on the
window-sill and on the little table inside; she paid most
attention to the fragrant yellow-blossomed musk, but did
not neglect the fuchsias nor the red daisies. Now and
again she would look across the narrow street to the house
opposite. Its window, which was on a level with the one
she looked from, was without shade or blind, and she saw
a young man, not much more than eighteen, sitting at a
table on which were many books and papers. There were
rocks too on the table and from time to time he would
break off a fragment of rock and begin examining it.

A great black cat came across the floor in the woman's
room, its tail erect. It leaped onto the chair beside her.
"You startled me, you black villain," she said. She sat
down by the window. The black cat leaped onto her
shoulder and began to purr, but her attention was on
neither the cat nor the yellow-blossomed musk, but on
the house opposite. The young man was still bent over
the books and quizzing the rocks, but the woman at the
window did not mind him. She was looking at the men at
work outside the house. They had a ladder to the wall
and a man on top. They had put up a new sign on the
house and were looking to see if the job had been done
correctly. The old one taken down had been left lying

168

against the wall. The woman at the window read the name on it:

MICHAEL KIRWAN
CORN MERCHANT

A woman came out of the house opposite, and gave the new sign a sharp look. She was wearing widow's weeds. She was satisfied with the work. Her own name was on the new sign: her dead husband's name was on the old one. The old sign was put into a cart and the horse moved steadily down the street.

But the woman did not move from the window. She was weary. She was very active in the course of the day. For she had a good trade, one very useful to the public. When people in the City were in difficulty, when they had the old sad story to tell — no work, no money, no food, no everything — she was much in demand. She would be in the way of helping them; a man with a good shirt or a woman with shoes that were not too worn, they need not lack for money as long as she was in the City.

Was she then a generous woman? She was not, but a decent woman with little printed tickets saying in white and red how much the person she helped had to pay. *Ma tante* the French would call her; "my Uncle" the English would call her. In the City she was known only as Nell. There was no danger of anyone looking for her going astray: he would see the three brass balls over her door.

Nell stayed at the window looking at the house of Kirwan and at the young man at his books, and at the new sign. In her nostrils was the fragrant perfume of the yellow musk and on her shoulder the great cat which she called "the black villain" was purring. But she was brooding.

Every night for nineteen years Nell would sit at this window looking over at the house of Kirwan and at the old trading sign. It seemed to her as if a great change had come on the world since she did not tonight see it. Despite herself, old memories came along. At first these old memories were without shape or form, like drizzle in the wind. But they were getting more exact gradually, until they were little clear pictures before her eyes, coming and going without relief.

She did not see the house beyond; she did not see the young student with his books and rocks; she did not see the new sign with the name of Kirwan's widow on it, even though it was that which set her first recollecting. But she did see a picture before her eyes. She did see a slender young man, with grey-blue eyes, humorous grey-blue eyes that were always laughing at the world. He is passing by the shop window, he looks in, just as she is looking out. He stands . . . . he looks at the articles in the window, he sees the young woman . . . .

But wasn't nineteen years a long time back?

The woman at the window got up. She went to the door. She took down a photograph hanging on the wall and examined it keenly by the light which came from the street. She sighed heavily. It was herself at seventeen. Although the photograph was old, and developed from a poor plate, anyone would know, without previous knowledge, that once Nell was good-looking. And he would not be far wrong if he said that the young man with the humorous grey-blue eyes would come back.

And he did. Didn't Nell see him now, although nineteen years had passed? She saw him now although she was looking at that student bent over his books.

He had come in one day when she herself was looking after the shop. How her heart leaped when she saw him! She had not indeed been expecting him.

He placed a watch on the counter.

"How much?" he said, and those were the first words she ever heard from him.

She told him.

"What's your name?" she said, pen in hand.

"Michael Kirwan."

She wrote it on a little ticket. Her cheeks flushed. She gave him the ticket and the money. He said something about his father not sending money in time, but his eyes were so lively and so mocking that the girl surmised his pockets were full.

Who was he? Who was the father that didn't send him money in time? What was he doing in the City? Such were the questions the young girl asked herself when he'd gone. She considered that it was herself he came to see, but having considered, only laughed. The girl liked his voice. And those humorous grey-blue lively eyes. And that curly hair. The girl hoped he would come again; she hoped his father would send him the money — to claim his watch. She thought it would be a great shame if he lost it. But of course he did not. He came again and again, and conveniently enough she was always in charge of the shop.

They met often after that: at early Sunday Mass in St John's Chapel; on the street when she was shopping; when she and her father went rowing on the lake on Sunday she would see him in his own boat. In May there was evening Rosary in the Chapel; he was there the second night — how would he know that she'd be there? But she became very friendly with Michael Kirwan . . .

The young student in the house across the way, with the new sign on it, got up; he stretched his arms; he looked in the direction of the window. Nell reared. O how like his father he was! . . . Although her eyes were fixed on the yellow-flowered musk it was of the day she went rowing on the lake with the father of the young student who was now stretching his arms that Nell was thinking. It was a fine sunny day at the beginning of summer. The land was in blossom. The lake like a great shining mirror of silver spread out from them on all sides. The small boat was moving through the water effortlessly, like a man on ice. He rowing; she at the helm. With each stroke of the oar he would throw himself back as if he were going from her, but would return on the next, and the two of them would laugh as if they were in agreement about something. And they were . . . . they both thought that youth was grand and that it was the only richness. Coming home in the evening . . . .

When the woman at the window had conjured up that much of the story, she got up and spoke aloud:

"'Would your father be agreeable?' he said.

"'He would,' I said.

"'And you yourself are agreeable, then?'

"'You're making fun of me!' I said."

The woman sat down again by the window.

"And he married Brigid Ruane and I and my family waiting at the Chapel!" she said bitterly. "Brigid was to blame. She stole him from me. But, Brigid . . . ." Nell got up and shook her fist at the house across the way and the young student. "May I not go to the grave, Brigid...."

She stopped herself; she saw Brigid Ruane, the widow of Kirwan, talking to the young student. He put away his books and his rocks. The look the young student gave to his mother went like a sharp knife into the heart of the woman opposite. The mother kissed him (her habit since she was widowed) and went off to bed.

In her own house Nell stayed by the window. The old memories which had been returning for two hours, but which went away again like chaff in the wind, were moulded and enforced and interwoven; her appearance was changed, and her nature; they were no longer old memories but reflections heavy with grief and hatred, except that every moment hatred was gaining on grief; she could not banish this hatred; she could not get away from it, and hatred begot vengeance. This vengeance, she thought, was something corporeal; a thing more terrible, more awful, more ugly than the father that begot it; to her it seemed a living thing, a malevolent thing, and she leaped up to fight it. She thrust out her hands to keep back this new enemy; there was a mighty contest; she left the room quickly; she threw herself on her knees before a little altar beside her bed; not a word came from her lips, but as she swayed to and fro before the altar, she herself was a prayer, a living prayer.

The enemy now was crushed, she thought . . . . but she woke up her maid, old Kate, with her bitter weeping.

In the morning Nell opened the shop as usual at half-past seven. A very occasional customer would come as early as that and if he did old Kate would make him stay until her mistress returned from eight o'clock Mass.

But this morning Nell had scarcely opened the shop when she saw a barefoot woman coming towards her across the street. She was a timid little woman, terror in her eyes. You would think by her gait, her weak mouth, the urgent look in her eyes, that she was fear itself in the form of a woman. She was one of the wretched little women seen among the poor of the big towns whose every action is an excuse for being alive at all. She carried an infant at her breast.

She placed the big bundle she was carrying before Nell, like one offering a sacrifice.

Nell would rather have seen the devil than this woman at such an hour of the morning. She bore her no ill-will, but she had to crush the enemy she had encountered while sitting by the window. Sending this woman to her before she went to Mass was part of the trickery of the enemy; had she not thought of the little woman's husband as the one who would aid her in getting satisfaction, in avenging herself on the Kirwans? He was a heavy drinker and if he and the young student became companions . . . . Look how his father went; if his mother let him, would he not kill himself with it? . . . . The craving was in the blood of the Kirwans she thought. But Brigid would not allow a drop across the threshold . . . .

Nell opened the bundle the other woman put on the counter. The first thing she came across was a very long, very white, very narrow-bodied robe, a robe for a new-born child. She put it on one side.

"Isn't he working?" Nell said to the little woman.

"Yes, but he's drunk all we have. He got a short leave . . . . he's been drinking for four days . . . . now, he's woken me up . . . . he'll raze the house on me if I don't get him a couple of glasses of whiskey."

Nell took a couple of sleeveless shirts from the bundle, so tiny they'd hardly fit a doll. She placed them beside the long white robe.

"Bad company," said Nell. "He wouldn't drink if it wasn't for the bad company."

She took out two pairs of bootees (Nell called them socks) from the bundle.

"I knitted them myself," said the little woman, "look at the lovely ribbons I put in them to keep them falling off his feet."

The infant tried to seize them but failed.

"Bad company," said Nell, throwing the bootees (or socks) on the long white robe.

The young student, Kirwan's son, went by the door.

"Look at that young man," said Nell, "he doesn't touch a drop, *he* doesn't mix with bad company."

Nell placed a little coat of blue flannel on top of the other items; a tiny little coat made to keep the cold from the soft, fragrant, sheeny flesh of His Majesty. He tried to grab it, but his mother wouldn't let him, for all it was his own coat.

"If it wasn't for the bad company I wouldn't have to come to you with these things . . . . if it wasn't for them he'd be happy going around the country collecting his plants and studying them," said the little woman in a faint voice.

Nell took out from the bundle a big white coverlet knitted to protect His Majesty from the wind and the rain. She saw the young student passing again by the door.

"There's small danger he'd drink much," said Nell, "if he were in the company of that young man . . . . the two of them going around the country together; he collecting his plants . . . ."

Nell could say no more. She had not intended to say even that much, but speech slipped out despite herself. The enemy was working at her; the great corporeal thing she thought she had subdued the night before was drawing near to her. If the young student became a companion of this woman's husband, it would not be long before both of them would be in bad company; it would not be long before the young student took a drop; not long before he had the venomous craving . . . . not long before his mother's heart was broken — she who had stolen the man from her. So Nell was thinking, but all she said was:

"I suppose you want the usual?"

"The usual," said the other woman, ". . . . but," she said, while Nell was giving her the money, "it'd be very hard to get them all back together."

"Leave it to me," said Nell. "I'll fix it up for you, just you see."

Nell did not intend to say it. She did not intend it, but the enemy was close to her, inflaming her. He was getting the better of her.

"If you do that for me," said the woman, "there's not a day as long as I live I won't say a prayer for you."

She went. Nell went back into the room which seemed to be vibrating. She went to put on her old cloak to go to eight Mass, as she had done for eighteen years, but when she took it down, her mouth compressed, she threw the cloak aside, and went upstairs.

She sat in the big chair by the window. She looked over at the house of Kirwan. The young student was in the room opposite, packing lunch and a device for rock-breaking in his bag. His mother was at the door of the house. Nell was thoughtful as she looked over at the two of them; the son upstairs, the mother at the door. Her countenance did not reveal whatever thoughts were in her head. She might only have been inhaling the perfume of the musk, she might only have been listening to the purr of "the black villain".

The Mass bell rang. Nell did not get up. She only clenched her lips.

After a while she started up. She went to the mirror that hung over the hearth. She looked at herself. She shook her head.

"O I am too old," she said to herself, "he is only eighteen."

She clenched her lips again. She stood for a little while as if listening to something. She took a step . . . . she stood again . . . . she took another step: and down the stairs with her. She seized the old sateen cloak that was greyish with age, she seized the little black hat with the bird's feather sticking up in it jauntily, and put them on. If there were people in the City who did not go to work until they saw Nell on her way to Mass, they were late this

morning, for they did not see her. If they had been at the
top of a little street near the lake, they would have seen
a dark little woman wearing an old cloak greyish with
age and a hat with a bird's feather sticking up in it
jauntily, and they would have seen this little woman enter
the house of the woman who had brought her the bundle
that morning.

That same night when the shop was closed, Nell was
at the window. She saw two men making down the street,
each carrying a bag. One of them was the young student,
and the other man did not leave him until he reached the
door. The husband of that woman who had brought her
the bundle that morning . . . .

The pleasure of a swimmer who hesitates at the edge
of the water for fear it will be too cold and then finds that
inside it is not cold at all — such was Nell's pleasure
when she saw those two together. She laughed . . . . and
if she woke old Kate that night it was not with bitter
weeping.

Victory for the enemy.

Nell loved goats' milk. Every Sunday after eleven Mass,
she would strike out and take the road westwards along
the lakeside. She would be wearing the old sateen cloak
and the hat with the bird's feather sticking up in it
jauntily; when there was rain she would have an umbrella
open; she would have the same umbrella open when the
sun was very hot. She would not speak a word to anyone,
but always continued on until she reached a small house
beside the lake, about two-and-a-half miles from the City.
She would go in and drink a glass of goats' milk; if the
weather was fine, she would settle on the chair outside
the door, she would stay a while watching the boats
moving by, and she would drink another glass of the milk.

Many were the boats that landed there, and many the

glasses of goats' milk drunk in that small house beside the lake. Many also were the glasses of "milk" that came from no goat that were drunk there, if the man of the house knew those who drank it.

The next Sunday that Nell was sitting outside the door, drinking a second glass of goats' milk, when she saw two small boats contesting each other. There was only one man in each boat. The man in one of the boats was big, strong, and bulky; in the other boat was a slender young man but he was a better and more clever rowsman than the big man. Some of those watching them thought the big man would win the bet, others that the slender nimble man would succeed; he would have too, only one of his oars broke just opposite the small house.

He came ashore. So did the other man, and they both went into the small house. Nell recognized them. It was the young student, son of Kirwan, and the comrade she herself had chosen for him.

The young student thought he could borrow an oar from the man of the house. There were none.

The two men sat inside, near the door. They asked the man of the house for goats' milk. He knew the big man of old. If the drink they got had the colour of milk, it had not the smell of milk. They drank the second glass. The big man drank a third.

Since Nell was outside, she could not see them, but she heard everything they said.

"I'd have won the bet," said the young student, "if the oar hadn't let me down."

"You would . . . . but bad cess to you, drink another one—it's a sweltering day."

"I won't . . . . but you didn't see the wonderful stone I found in the Giant's Cave . . . ."

"A small one, have a small one, and we'll be going."

"Look at this stone," said the young student, "I never

saw its like before . . . . it's like granite, but you'd imagine there's a streak of limestone in it. Look . . . . thousands and thousands of years ago, this stone was in the womb of the earth . . . ."

"I'll have another one . . . . it's a sweltering day."

He drank another glass but Nell didn't know if the young student drank a third. If he did or not, it seemed to her he'd had his fill when he came out. When the big man saw the woman sitting outside the door, he greeted her. He knew her well.

"Are you going home?" he said.

"Yes," she said.

"You'd better come along with us in the boat."

The three set off in one boat: the two men rowing and she at the helm. Looking at the young student, her mouth clamped down. She had not been in a boat since she was on the lake with his father that day so long ago . . . . before he was born. She didn't know what possessed her to go with them . . . she gazed at that young man in front of her, that young man who with every stroke of the oar was going from her and coming towards her . . . . and his grey-blue eyes! Would they be so bright and shining had he not had a drop taken? Hadn't he the great chat? Wouldn't it be he who would yet write the important book on the rocks of the region? Nell couldn't help looking at him; wasn't he face to face? How like his father he was, going from her and coming towards her with every stroke of the oar, and the lake like a silver mirror spread out around them on every side . . . . but his father hadn't drunk a drop that day . . . . Nell herself might well have taken a drop, her eyes flaming, her cheeks flushed, that hat with the bird's feather sticking up in it jauntily askew on her head . . . .

A great rain-cloud caught them before they landed and the three were drenched.

"Wasn't I the foolish one to let you hide that bottle of whiskey on me this morning," said the big man. "We're wet to the skin now."

When they landed, the young scholar went to an old boat abandoned at the lakeside. The other two followed. He lifted a board at the head of the boat and the big man's bottle was found underneath. The two men took a swig from it.

The board was on the ground at Nell's feet. On the lower part she made out letters cut by a knife. She looked at them closely

M. K.
N. B.
1888

were the letters on the board. M.K. i.e. Michael Kirwan, N.B. i.e. Nell Browne; the day they decided to marry was the day they cut those letters on the board, that day when the lake was a silver lake spread out all round them and the bloom of youth was on them both. . . .

She flung the board into the lake and looked at the two men who were drinking.

That night when Nell was sitting at the window watering the plants, she looked across at the house of Kirwan. It was not the young student she saw in the room opposite but his mother, and she was shedding tears.

A month had not gone by when the young student visited Nell. He came when night was falling, as if he were afraid to be seen.

He took a bracelet from his pocket.

"I want some money," he said, "to buy books."

Nell looked at the bracelet. It was a valuable one.

"From Michael Kirwan to his wife Brigid" were the words inscribed inside.

"My mother hadn't the money to give me today," said the young man. "She'd a quarter's rent to pay."

Nell gave him three pounds, although she would not give a penny to anyone else for a bracelet with a name inscribed.

"I'll come back for it in a couple of days," he said.

When the shop was closed that night Nell went upstairs. She sat in the chair by the window. She looked over at the house of Kirwan. She saw Brigid in the room opposite. She put the bracelet on her arm. She began to walk back and forward. She was deeply moved. She began to talk to herself. Should he not have given her the bracelet at the start? Would he not have given it to her but for you, Brigid Ruane? Does the man in the grave know that the bracelet he gave his wife is on my arm? If he does is he angry?

She was at the window. She looked over. The woman was in the room opposite.

"He knows it, he knows it, Brigid Ruane! He'd rather it were on my arm than yours. . . . Michael Kirwan! Michael Kirwan! Would it not be on my arm from the beginning if she hadn't put a spell on you? Give me a sign, Michael Kirwan, that so it would have been without that one. Give me the sign Michael, Michael darling, and I'll be satisfied. . . .I'll not interfere with your son. . . .I'll give him good advice, Michael, if only you give me the sign. . . ."

She fancied that the bracelet was lying very heavily on her wrist. It seemed to her the old house was vibrating, that she sensed it creaking, and beneath a great swaying.

The great black cat came across the floor, its tail erect. It rubbed against Nell's foot. She started. She almost fainted. . . .

She sat again at the window. There wasn't a soul to be seen on the street. It was getting late. Now and again a man would go by; a sailor going to his ship or a boatman come ashore on the evening tide. From time to time Nell would look over at the house of Kirwan, and she would see the woman's face at the window, but when the woman saw the woman opposite she would draw aside. When the woman opposite looked again, she would see the other woman's face there, every now and then looking up and down the street.

Finally the two women heard song. It was a man singing. The two women looked out. They saw each other, but neither of them drew back her head. They both recognized the voice. They both saw the young student approaching, and he was staggering. The woman across the way blessed herself and left the window. The other woman did not leave until she saw the two of them at the door, the son and the mother, the mother trying to coax her son in.

And not one night, but every night in the week, the two women would be waiting until the young man came home. A bracelet on the arm of one of them; the perfume of the fragrant musk in her nostrils; the big cat on her shoulder; iniquity in her heart, and hope that he'd come home more drunk than the night before. The other woman white-faced and hoping to God it would not be long before her son came home. When the two women saw each other, it was the mother who would draw aside, but when they heard the singing approach, they would both look in its direction, and they would see the young student coming, and he would be staggering.

By this time the young student cared little for his books and rocks; that woman with the great black cat on her shoulder cared little for eight Mass. Now she went only to Sunday Mass.

But one night Nell was not wearing the bracelet. She went into the shop to get it, to put on for a while at the window, but it was not there. She searched everywhere. She did not find it. But if she did not, she found a knife, a long crooked knife with a broken blade; it was beside the box where she kept the bracelet. She had an idea who lost the knife, stole the bracelet. She brought the long crooked knife to the constables. Within two days the young student was arrested.

The night he was arrested Nell was in a little room at the back of the house, looking to see if anything else was missing. Many a tale attached to the objects that lay before the little woman; to each one a history belonged that would reveal a good deal about life among the poor in the City. She had the place in a turmoil when the young student's mother came in. Nell was astonished. She didn't know how she got in, since she thought she had locked the door; she didn't even know that the young student had been arrested.

The mother threw herself on her knees in front of the other woman.

"O don't make a thief of him! Don't make a thief of him in front of the world!" she said.

"He made a thief of himself," said Nell.

"Don't say anything against him, O don't say. . . .it would be a shame to say he stole it. . . .he didn't! My son never stole anything. . . .but he was ashamed when I found out the bracelet was gone. . . .he was ashamed I should think he had sold it — I gave him the money to give you. . . .I gave it to him twice, three times but. . . .but. . . .but he drank it. . . . Say he didn't steal it. . . .say you gave it to him yourself. . . . Say anything. . . .in the name of God and His Blessed Mother. . . . My darling son, what a plight you're in **tonight**. . . .and he's only nineteen. . . ."

The mother had a grip on the other woman's dress so that she could not escape. The other woman was looking at the tormented white face beneath her. She compressed her lips.

"Your son was old enough to steal what belonged to me, Brigid Ruane," said the other woman.

"To steal what belongs to you. . . ." said the mother; she was about to say "the bracelet Michael Kirwan gave", she remembered herself in time.

"Yes, to steal what belongs to me," said the other woman, "didn't I lend him money on it?"

"You did, you did. . . .but I'll give you your money. . . . I'll give it to you seventeen fold. . . . I'll give you everything I have but don't send him to prison. Don't send him and I'll give you everything I have and my blessing with it. . . . I'll go begging. . . ."

The other woman tried to escape but the mother had a tenacious grip on her. There was only a candle in the room and two shadows might be seen on the whole wall at the back: A woman on her knees swaying to and fro; the other woman standing like a post, looking down on the woman who was kneeling. In the chimney of that old house which was built in the Spanish style, the west wind which came across the bay and the streets of the City from the great sea was having a high old time.

"I gave him money for the bracelet. I gave it to him for what belonged to me," said the woman who was standing, and in her voice was the force of the west wind, "but if the man in the grave were present here tonight, Brigid Ruane, he'd tell us that he should have given it to me in the first place. . . .and he'd tell us he would have given it to me if it hadn't been for the spell you put on him, Brigid Ruane. . . ."

The kneeling woman started. Her grip softened a little.

"There was the mean streak in your son's heart from

the beginning, Brigid Ruane," said the woman who was standing, "and he didn't pick it up off the ground. . . .he didn't get it from his father Brigid Ruane. . . . Who stole the man from me and he on the point of marrying me, Brigid Ruane? Many a day for the last nineteen years I said to myself that I would not rest easy in my grave if I did not see the woman who did that on me on her knees before me, before I parted this life. . . . Now, Brigid Ruane!"

The mother was about to rise from her knees, but she gave one glance at the standing woman, imploring her to give her back her son. The west wind began to whistle and cavort in the chimney of the old house. The candle was almost quenched.

"My son! My son!" said the mother, and the extent of her grief would have moved anyone. . . . "My son! My son!" she said. . . . "Don't keep him from me!"

But that night the other woman's heart was a stone.

"You might as well be talking to the wall," she said, and she turned her back.

The mother stayed for a moment watching her.

"May the curse of mothers who lost their children fall on you," she said, "may it follow you through this life, and await you in the next!" and she went out.

The other woman did not stir. The west wind which came from the great sea across the bay and the city streets began again to whistle and cavort in the chimney; it came down through the chimney and went around the floor to escape through the door which had been left open. The candle was quenched.

The young student got a prison sentence. He would have got longer had it not come out at the hearing that there was no one in Nell's shop the day he went there to give her the money and get the bracelet; that he saw it lying around; that he snatched it up without thinking and was afraid to return. Nell had to admit that she used spend the night at the window.

But she did not spend it so any more, and she never again wore the dress she had on that night. The marks of the other woman's fingers were on it.

It rained heavily the day the young student came out of prison. When the shop was closed Nell went upstairs; and she sat at the window though the only light in the room came from a street lamp standing at the corner of the house. The perfume of the musk was in her nostrils; the big cat was on her shoulder, trying to be friendly with her. She looked over at the house of Kirwan, thinking she might see the young student in the room opposite. He was not there. He was visiting a friend, although his mother was begging him to stay at home. But he promised her he would not stay out long and would not let a drop pass his lips. . . .

Nell knew that he would be in the room if he were at home. She drove away the big cat. She was somehow afraid that he would begin drinking again. She had got satisfaction. She put the son in prison and the mother on her knees. But he couldn't be drinking — perhaps he had gone to bed. . . .

She got up. She took the bracelet from the box in which she'd put it the day the constables returned it. She went to the window and looked across, and in her hand was that bracelet which Michael Kirwan of the grey-blue eyes had given to his wife. She stayed at the window a long time looking across. . . .

A light was lit in the room opposite. Nell saw the papers and books and rock specimens the young student had left on the the table; they had not been stirred while he was in prison. She saw Brigid Ruane in the room, going back and forward, back and forward, without pause. She saw her sitting at the window, all the time looking up and down the street. She saw her pale anguished face, but when the woman saw her, she would go from the window. And when the other woman saw her going, she had a keen impulse to go to her, to offer her the bracelet in her hand, and beg for forgiveness. But she did not go, although she had subdued the hatred in her heart.

The big city clock began to strike; one, two, three. . . eleven o'clock. The two women counted and looked out. Neither drew back her head. It was pouring rain, and the west wind was driven before it through the narrow streets of the City. Paper and sticks and other rubbish was sweeping down the street. Nell saw a piece of orange skin being driven past the street lamp at the corner of the house. Being agitated herself, she took note of every detail. There were lights in many other windows in the street, but they were going out one by one.

The big clock began to strike again; one, two, three. . . .twelve o'clock.

Nell felt pity for the woman opposite. She made to tread on the wretched bracelet. She took it up again; she went at a run to the door to go over to the other woman. She stopped. She returned to the window. The adversary was still close to her.

The big clock began to strike again; one. . . .only one stroke, but that stroke put terror in the hearts of both women. Both were hoping they would see before long the son of that man who once had humorous grey-blue eyes but was now under the clay. . . .

The moon appeared. The street was gleaming wet and slippery after the rain.

The big clock began to strike again; one, two. Two strokes. The two women looked at each other. Two sailors were passing by. The woman opposite put her head outside the window:

"Did you see my son anywhere?" she said, but before they had time to answer, she was gone from the window.

The big clock started: one, two, three. . . . The two women looked at each other.

They heard some noise or other. They both listened carefully. What was it? It was coming closer. . . .but it was only the creaking of a dray. It passed between the two houses and it seemed to the two women that the driver was asleep and the two horses were trying to make the way home. It was a distillers' dray.

The big clock started: one, two, three, four. . . . The two women looked at each other. A sound came to them on the west wind. They saw the young student coming, and he was staggering. He stood at the top of the street to let the dray go by. . . . The horses were proceeding steadily. . . .he decided to cross the street. . . .he slipped. . . .the two women screeched. . . .the dray was on top of him.

It is said in the City that he would still be alive if he had not stood on that piece of orange skin; but other people think he was tired of himself and of his life. . . .

Nell is still seen at the window, the great black cat on her shoulder, and the perfume of musk in her nostril. But when she looks across the narrow street she does not see any of the Kirwans in the house opposite. They all rest in a single grave, in the Churchyard of St. John.

Farewell Friends

translated by Val Mulkerns

Now that the cold wet torment of winter is upon us again, and the calm pleasures of summer no more, I have to say farewell to a host of my old friends, the little living creatures of woods and lonely places. I have to head in the direction of snug houses and all that goes with them until we've put the cold and frost behind us once more.

But the way it is with me I have the feeling I'm betraying the old quarry by undertaking this trip to the city. How can the likes of me take easily to feather beds and soft white sheets again, to all the easy luxury of city life, after the spell of three seasons that I've spent under the skies of heaven?

I'll never forget you, old quarry! I'll never forget the strong ties of comradeship that I made with my fellow creatures and I living in that lovely place. I'll never forget those starry nights with nothing between me and the overpowering sky only the thin mantle of air that drifts around this world of ours. No night I ever spent like that seemed long, even though I was many a time without a wink of sleep between starshine and morning's light. How would the time seem long with all those friends of the night around me? Wasn't it there I made close acquaintance with the squirrel and the weasel and the fieldmouse, with the small baby rabbit that came looking for alms? I got to know you and your ways thoroughly by day and

189

by night and if we quarrelled itself in the end over the thievery of that weasel, which of you would say the fault was mine alone?

And listen, you feathered tribes, I have to take my leave of you too and give you thanks, songsters and silent alike, for all you gave me by way of pleasure this year that's gone from us. Don't blame me for deserting you! Isn't it a pity and a heartscald that a man like me can't survive winter among the friends he made during the summer? But even if it is natural for you feathered folk to live out the winter in bush and thicket, I know even so that it often goes hard with you when the cruel weather strikes.

Farewell friends, until the spring comes, until the yellow summer follows after.

And listen, who knows but I might rob a handful of grain from time to time from some farmer to keep you going throughout the winter. . . .

*

As for you, little black donkey, I suppose I'll have to take my leave of you too. The fierce winter is coming on us and it wouldn't be too good for either of us to be travelling the roads of Ireland in that season of frost and rain. You'll be in some nice snug barn until the spring comes around again. You'll be neither cold nor hungry, however I may fare. . . .

It goes hard with me to part with the little black donkey even for a while itself. I loved him from the first footsore day I set eyes on him at the fair of Kinvara. It wasn't for the colour of his coat or the sturdy bulk of him or the eyes or the charming ears or the little pretty feet that I took to him. It wasn't for his speedy legs either, for pace or prance were no part of his nature. It was for his personality alone, and I don't think anybody could fail to love him for that. Wouldn't he melt the heart even of the knight of the broken pots himself!

But farewell now, friend, until we set course again next spring for the plains of your favourite thistles!

Of course I have friends other than the creatures I've mentioned, human friends that I never meet up with except when I'm out in the wilderness. I have to say farewell to them too. I hadn't time in the course of this book to make reference to Peadar and Sean and Seamus, three young fellows I used to meet every morning when I was by myself in the wood. They mostly couldn't spend too much time with me because of having to be about their work earning money for their families, but I'll remember till the day I die the **feast of** sport we'd have together in the heart of the leafy **woods**. The stories we'd tell under the trees!

I hear the voice of the young storyteller in my ears this minute and he telling us about the Pooka: "It was an angel he was in the beginning. . . ." I can still see the boy's bright eyes and he speaking: "An angel he was that went to war with God, but he wasn't thrown down into hell — he wasn't thrown down because he did some good deed some time before this, and therefore he was given leave to live in four places in Ireland. . . ."

Another lad didn't believe a word of it. How would it be true, when he'd never seen the thing himself? Thomas was the nickname I put on that lad the next time we met . . . . But farewell to you too, young human friends, until the spring comes!

*

As for you, knight of the road, is it possible I won't see you again for three or four months? I know we may meet inside in the town, but wouldn't anybody with a shred of judgement or understanding know that there's a big difference between a knight of the road that you'd see in town and the gallant pacing fellow making his own living for himself out in the wilderness.

To him and to all you gentry of the roads of Ireland I say farewell until the skies clear and the rough winter is gone and the hot bright tranquil days of endless summer are with us once more in Ireland.